SHADOW

Book 2 of the Misfit

C. S. Churton & Keira Stone

Other Titles By C.S Churton

Druid Academy Series
DRUID MAGIC
FERAL MAGIC
PRIMAL MAGIC

Druid Enforcer Academy Series
FAMILIAR MAGIC

Fur 'n' Fang Academy Series
MOON BITTEN
CURSE BITTEN
FERAL BITTEN

Misfit Magic Academy Series
SHADOW CHARMED
SHADOW CURSED
SHADOW CHAOS

TalentBorn Series
AWAKENING
EXILED
DEADLOCK
UNLEASHED
HUNTED
CHIMERA

Chapter One

I'd never wanted to be back at Braeseth as badly as I did right now. It wasn't that I really enjoyed being at the academy—because seriously, not *that* much could change in a year. It was tough when most of my magic was frankly awful, and I was almost certain all the knowledge I'd crammed into my brain for my end-of-year exams had vanished the moment the semester had finished. Still, it was better than the alternative.

Leaving the house had become nearly impossible over summer, thanks to my parents finally realising they had a daughter, and one who wasn't presently incarcerated in prison at that. But I'd finally convinced them that I needed to head to Fantail Market and buy things for my return to Braeseth, which was an excuse they couldn't argue with, since apparently I now represented the family's entire magical future. Hell, I'd even done some shopping once I got here, and I had a half dozen new textbooks to show for my trouble. But the real reason I was here was to catch up with Eva, my roommate from Braeseth, and only real friend in the world. I tapped my foot against the table leg as I anxiously scanned every face for signs of her. It had been agony not getting to see her since the end of last semester.

"Norah!"

My ears perked up at the sound of her voice and I practically leapt out of my seat. I stopped short of throwing my arms around her and holding on for dear life. I didn't need to give people yet another reason to talk about me.

"You made it," I said, standing awkwardly by the table.

"Of course I did," she said with a grin, and sat down at the table opposite me.

Relief washed over me with dizzying speed. Sometimes, late at night, I'd almost convinced myself she had only tolerated me last year. I really should not be left alone with my thoughts. It never ended well.

"So, how've you been?" I asked, propping my chin in both hands.

"Missing my best friend," she answered with a genuine smile. "But summer was okay."

"How are things going with your mum's search?" Last I'd heard, her mother was still trying to track down Eva's biological father. Given that her magic came from his bloodline, her mum had decided it made sense to know as much as they could about the man. And probably to avoid scammers trying to dupe her daughter—which was exactly what had nearly happened when Eva's lie-detecting ability first manifested and she decided to go looking by herself.

She sighed and tugged at one of the slender twists of hair over her shoulder. "She's still looking. Thought she might have tracked him to France, but that went cold."

"That's rough. I know it's kind of been a thing for her for a while."

"I don't even know what I'll do if I meet him. I know I went looking first, but I put that aside, you know? Or I thought I had. And I just don't want to make a fool of myself."

I snorted. "As if. You are brilliant, and *he* would have to be the fool not to see it."

She ducked her head, her hair falling like tiny ribbons over her face. "Can we talk about something else? What about you? How was your summer?"

I let out a groan. "I thought living in Micah's shadow at home was bad. Turns out, doing something worth noticing is worse."

"Come on, it can't be that bad. I thought you wanted them to realise you existed."

"I did. I mean, I thought I did. But they just keep staring at me, like they're expecting me to do something. Not that I've got any idea what. Honestly, it's kind of creeping me out." I exhaled heavily. "I don't know, maybe they're scared of what I did, but they've barely let me leave the house since I got back after last semester."

"So, no sneaking around with a certain druid enforcer who fancies you?"

Heat burned in my cheeks at the mention of Zachary. "No, I haven't seen him since the semester ended. Which is probably for the best, because I'm pretty sure me turning up with a druid in tow—and an enforcer, at that—would have pushed my parents over the edge. Anyway, it's probably not going to go anywhere. He's back working his regular assignment. And given what's been going on, I can't imagine Bevan would want enforcers back on campus."

"I keep telling you, Norah, stop selling yourself short with him. He likes you. It's obvious to anyone with eyeballs. Let him flirt with you. Let him ask you out on a date. Hell, let him kiss you senseless."

My lips tingled at the memory of my first kiss with him. I'd never been the type to make the first move with a guy, and yet I'd been the one leaning in and kissing him. Of course, the moment had then been somewhat ruined by two other enforcers faking an attack so they could hide runes all over the academy, but it was what it was.

"I'll think about it," I finally mumbled.

"Because I can find reasons to be other places," she said with a wink.

"I did convince my parents to let me leave the house one other time," I blurted.

"Yeah? For what?"

"The Circle's trial." I wasn't sure why this topic had jumped to the forefront of my mind.

Eva glanced at the coffee shop beside us and gestured toward it. "While I won't say no to hearing how Celine and her lapdogs did facing the consequences of their actions, I'm going to need some fortification. You want anything?"

"Just a black coffee. Thanks." I reached into my pocket, but she waved me off.

"My treat."

I watched her as she disappeared into the shop, and slumped back in my chair. I tried not to picture the trial or its aftermath in my head. I hadn't been asked to give evidence, and the Council had kept their word. That was all I should be focusing on. I'd done everything I said I'd do to keep them honest. And besides, it was better for me to just focus on the year ahead. With any luck—not that I tended to be particularly lucky—everyone would have forgotten the fact the academy had nearly been drained of magic a few months ago.

Given my mum and dad's constant vigilance around me since I'd got home, I hadn't practiced much with my magic. Probably not the best thing when I was still struggling to get caught up with everyone else in my year. I'd been too afraid that any accidents would be used as evidence that I was turning into my brother, and I didn't need them deciding that having me around was too much of a risk to what remained of their precious reputation, and handing me over to the authorities.

A little practice now probably wasn't such a bad thing. Even though I was sitting here in the open, it felt safer than my room at home. People were going about their own lives, oblivious to the girl who could manipulate shadows. I wasn't important to them, and while some people despised being obscure and unrecognised, to me it was comforting. Especially after a summer of living under the microscope.

I took in a slow breath, exhaling it through my nose and focused on the tips of my fingers. I could feel the slick surface of the table beneath them and tried to hold onto that sensation in my sense memory. When I lifted my fingers from the table, they could still sense the coolness they'd just left. Turning my hands over, I cupped my palms together, envisioning the shadows pooling there with the texture and constituency of silk. Too often when my magic came out, it was all plumes of smoke and darkness. I'd gotten lucky a few times last semester when it had wrapped around me like fabric. I longed for that sensation again. I wasn't sure why, but it felt like I had more control that way.

Nothing happened. Even though I could still feel the

texture of the table on my fingertips and I'd centred my body, the magic refused to obey.

"Come on," I whispered through gritted teeth.

Pulling my hands apart, I clenched them into fists, flexing my fingers a few times and blew out another slow breath. I couldn't be that out of practice, could I?

"Remember how your magic feels." Instructor Glover's voice echoed in my head, reminding me of the lessons we'd shared on Saturday mornings for months.

This time, I let my hands hand down by my sides and closed my eyes. In the blankness of my mind's eye, I pictured shadows rolling in, like thick storm clouds full of the anxiety and anger that had shaped me for so long. The doubt that I could ever be any good at this whole magic thing. In my mind, my hands reached toward the anxiety clouds, beckoning them to bend to my will. Slowly, painfully so, they turned into little funnels, spiralling down to perch on each fingertip.

My whole body went still as I tried to keep the funnels drifting down. I didn't want to ruin the moment or risk breaking the momentum by opening my eyes. I could almost feel the magic lacing itself around my fingers like a glove. It tightened its hold on me, begging me to give it purpose and direction.

"Still can't even control her magic. How pathetic."

Celine's voice carved through the mental imagery and

I opened my eyes to find her and her cronies dogging her heels. A liquid-like pool of darkness dripped from my fingers so that they looked like I'd stuck them in a vat of tar. So much for my silk glove.

The girls standing next to my table wore sneers that did not bear any resemblance to the looks of fear and uncertainty that they'd had when I'd seen them last. They'd cowered together beneath the Circle's orders, sending them to prison. True to their word, the Council had given them a lenient sentence—only six weeks—and in a minimum-security facility. All things considered, they'd gotten off easy.

"Didn't realise they let you out," I said, trying to keep my tone even, unemotional.

Celine leaned in, doing her best to tower over me even though we were about the same height. The look of disdain on her face contrasted with her vibrant red hair, and a chill spread down my spine that had no business being there. After all, I'd bested her last Halloween. And I'd been able to take on a druid where she'd failed.

"Did you think we'd forget what you did to us? You must be so pleased with yourself. Got away with everything, got to be the hero."

"I didn't ask for any of that," I snapped. "And all I did was tell the truth. You should be thanking me."

"Thanking you? You ruined my life, Norah," Celine

hissed, her hands balling into tight, white-knuckled fists. "Because of *you*, no one is going to want to touch me. I have a record. Do you have any idea how hard it's going to be to get anywhere after graduation?" She barely stopped long enough for me to open my mouth before she continued her tirade. "No, of course you didn't. You just thought about yourself. You selfish bitch."

"I saved your life and your magic, or did that part slip your memory? And maybe you should have considered what would happen before you tried to sabotage the entire academy."

A tingle spread over my hands and arms, and I looked down to find them black up to the elbows. Sure, now, when I didn't want it, my magic came easy.

Maybe she was remembering our fight on last Halloween too, or maybe she was still on edge from being in prison, but Celine's hands flew up, electricity rippling over her arms, ready to strike. I was out of my chair, shadows undulating around me ready to solidify and protect me from any attack.

"You should have just kept your dumb mouth shut," she snarled. "We were trying to make things better."

I didn't have the patience to stand here and debate this with her. I didn't need to justify my actions to her. And if she couldn't handle the consequences of her actions, that wasn't my fault. I had half a mind to just leave—I had no desire to get arrested for property damage or fighting—but I'd come here to enjoy spending time with my best friend. I wasn't about to abandon Eva. And I wasn't about to let Celine ruin my first day of freedom in forever.

Celine took my moment of hesitation for what it was and lobbed an energy ball at me. I raised my hands and the shadows swallowed her magic, extinguishing it like a flame. She let out a grunt and formed another energy ball.

"Why don't you piss off and leave her alone," a male voice called off to our right.

Celine and I turned in unison to find a guy who looked vaguely familiar standing there. He wore a button down short-sleeved shirt and dark grey trousers. The spat with Celine was nearly pushed from my mind as I tried to place him. The freckles peppered across his cheeks looked like they should form a constellation. And there was definitely something familiar about the vibrant blue shade of his eyes. But for the life of me, I couldn't figure out where I'd seen him before. Maybe he just worked around here. I hadn't exactly been frequenting Fantail Market this summer, but it wasn't like I'd never been before.

Celine clearly recognised him and decided his presence was too much of an inconvenience. She gave me one last sneer then pivoted and flounced off, her lackeys in tow. Her magic trailed after her, leaving the scent of ozone in her wake.

"Thanks," I said to the guy still standing there, hands in his pockets.

"She shouldn't have attacked you."

I shrugged. "Honestly, it wasn't the first time."

He shifted his weight from foot to foot and the way he chewed his lower lip suggested he had more to say. But his initial bravado vanished and he couldn't meet my gaze.

"See you around," he said and darted away.

I sank back into my seat and rubbed my forehead, trying to stave off a headache I could already feel forming right behind my eyes. I heard a door off to my left open and close, the tiny chime of a bell signalling someone either entering or leaving, and footsteps approached. I sat up to find Eva sitting back down across from me with our coffees.

"Sorry, that took a century. This lady in front of me changed her order six times. No joke."

I snatched the cup of coffee she'd set in front of me and downed it. The caffeine pushed the headache away and I sighed. When I set the cup down, I found Eva eyeing me like I had three heads.

"Okay, I clearly missed something. Spill."

I shook my head. "It was nothing. Just some old

drama trying to come back to haunt me."

Her eyebrows arched in an I-don't-believe-you expression, but she didn't say more. I expected her to pepper me with questions about the trial, after all, that was the whole reasons she'd gone to get coffee, but we just sat there in the cool breeze, enjoying each other's company.

"I can't believe I'm about to say this, but I am actually looking forward to being back on academy grounds," I said half an hour later as we headed off, ready to part ways for just a few more hours. At least I had the fact that we'd be roommates again to look forward to.

"Come on, after everything that happened last semester, this year is going to be easy," Eva said with a friendly smile and affectionate shoulder nudge.

She just had to say it, didn't she?

Chapter Two

The next day, I prepared myself for the gut-wrenching task of stepping foot back on the academy grounds. Not because I was nervous about being back among my fellow students—well not *just* because I was nervous about that—but literal gut wrenching. I hated those stupid portal stones. I'd half hoped Zachary would appear just to get me there and cover for me while I retched in the bushes. No such luck. Despite what he'd said at the end of last semester, he clearly had no interest in seeing me again.

So, I hunkered down by the tree Eva and I had claimed as ours last year and waited for my stomach to settle. Thankfully, the foliage was thick enough to cover me from most prying eyes. Wiping my mouth with the back of my hand, I straightened up and sucked in a few breaths of air. The queasiness was passing faster than it had the last time I'd travelled this way. Maybe I was getting more used to the magic. I didn't see why they couldn't just take down the wards for the day so we could all get in and out using an actual portal—which came with none of the side effects of the stones. Okay, so it was true, I didn't actually know *how* to open a portal, but they could have sent one for me and the rest of the magically inept, right?

"You okay?" Eva's voice penetrated the tree cover as she stepped through, one of the long twists in her hair catching on a branch. She swatted it away, tugging her hair free so she could reach me.

"I hate those portal stones," I grumbled and sat down on top of my suitcase.

"That explains the hiding," she said and sat beside me, draping an arm around my shoulders in a show of camaraderie.

"Yeah, well, I don't need the whole academy knowing I've got a weak stomach. I'd never hear the end of it." I sighed and rubbed at my temples. "I guess we'd better go inside. Won't do to miss Bevan's start of semester address."

Staying under the radar meant being where people expected me to be when they expected me to be there. They were less likely to notice me if I didn't give them a reason. We both stood and dragged my case out from under the foliage. As we trudged up the front steps into the entry hall, I wondered what classes awaited us this semester. I vaguely recalled Instructor Rathbone mentioning something about Runes, but I had no idea if that was a required course or an elective. And if it wasn't required, did I really want to be choosing things, giving people more reason to notice me? Not to mention the added workload, because honestly I'd struggled enough last year without signing up for extra classes.

As if he knew I'd been thinking of him, Instructor Rathbone stepped up, intercepting us before we could get much beyond the front doors. "Welcome back, ladies."

"Thanks, sir," Eva said, flashing him a smile.

"I hope you had a good summer holiday." His gaze was laser-focused on me. His beard looked fuller than last I'd seen him and somehow it made him look even more intense.

"Uh, I mean I didn't consume anything in shadow, so I suppose that's good?" Somehow, it came out as a question. Ugh. Just being back here was already making me doubt myself. More so than usual, that was.

"I hope you've been practicing. Energy Manipulation is first block Monday morning. I look forward to seeing you both there bright and early." He clapped his hands and grinned for effect before he wandered off to greet other students, his hair wound into a knot on the top of his head.

"That was weird," Eva whispered in my ear.

She'd taken the words right out of my mouth. I shrugged—I had other concerns. "Do you think we have to take our cases upstairs ourselves before the speech?" I eyed the suitcase dubiously, because if I'd suspected there might be actual heavy lifting involved, I was pretty sure

I'd have found a way to do without some of those textbooks. I mean, how much studying did one person need to do, anyway?

I recognised some faces milling about as students from the year above us and a couple from our year, too. I didn't see anyone who looked like the incoming class of first years. I guess they did it that way so that we didn't scare the hell out of the new students. If any of them were half as reluctant as I'd been, just being here would be overwhelming, without having the rest of the academy staring at them. Of course, I'd had to deal with that as well last year, and, well, it hadn't exactly been a barrel of laughs. I would have been even more intimidated if I'd seen the higher years sprawled out through the hall.

It was kind of jarring not to see the druids patrolling the corridor. I suspected they were staying far from the academy to avoid allegations that they weren't truly stepping out of our affairs. Still, the place felt a little empty without them.

Empty without a particular druid.

I pushed the thoughts of Zachary aside. There was no way he'd end up back here. He had his own life to live without getting dragged down by some student several years younger than him, and you could bet your life that wherever *he* was, he wasn't thinking about me. I turned my attention to trying to pick out more faces that I recognised. Across the hall I thought I spotted the guy from the market but he turned his back, engaging in conversation with someone else too quickly for me to get a good look.

"You look a bit lost, Miss Sheehan," Instructor Glover's voice cut through my musing.

It was like a bloody reunion. I pivoted to face her. "Just not sure what we're supposed to do with our cases."

"Ah, yes, I don't know why they don't send information on ahead of semester to avoid that sort of confusion. You'll leave them here and they'll be brought up during the dean's welcome speech."

"We aren't in the same dorms as last semester, though, are we?"

"Same general area, but no, you'll be one dormitory over. There should be a list on the door with room assignments."

"Oh, good. Thanks."

Her gaze narrowed and I fought the urge to shrink back. Even though I'd spent a lot of time in her company last semester, her scrutinising stare still made me want to turn invisible. "How was your summer?"

Why was everyone suddenly so interested in how I spent my holiday?

"Fine."

"Practice at all?"

I rubbed the nape of my neck and cast my gaze to the floor. "A little. It wasn't exactly easy to find time and privacy. But it's like riding a bike, right? Once you do it again a little, it comes back to you."

Instructor Glover sighed and the weight of her disappointment hit me like a tidal wave. "For some people, yes, but most students need to have consistent practice to keep and hone their skills. I would have thought, given how late you started, you'd have kept up the exercises we worked on in our sessions."

"I know. I should have done more, but I swear I'll be ready for class."

Her lips pressed into a thin line. It was clear she had her doubts, which was fair, because I shared them. "I'm going to hold you to that, Norah. You have such a beautiful gift. I'd hate to see you not use it to its full potential."

Off to my left, I heard the doors to the assembly hall open and someone clear their throat. Instructor Glover gestured that direction. "You'd better head in. Don't want to miss the start of semester welcome."

Given that it meant I would have to be with the rest of the students, I was almost certain I'd rather be anywhere else. As Eva and I settled in seats near the back—the better to make a quick exit—I noticed that people were actively avoiding the seats near us. And not just students from our year.

"Don't they know it's rude to stare?" Eva said, crossing her arms with a huff.

"They aren't staring at you," I muttered. Most people didn't even know that she'd been there when Celine and I had faced off with the druids. All they'd heard was that I had stopped Celine from doing something crazy and the druids from stealing our magic.

In any rational mind, that should make people want to be nice to me. Maybe even to thank me for what I'd done. Not that I wanted the praise. I'd be much happier if they all forget it had ever happened. But as I looked around the crowded space and met their gazes, I didn't need magic to sense their hostility. A red-haired guy who had to be in the year above of us glared so intensely I worried the crease in his forehead would become permanent. Then he leaned over to the girl next to him and whispered something. This prompted her to turn in her seat and make eye contact, too.

"What?" I mouthed at her.

She didn't answer. Just spun back around. The far door opened and Celine walked in. A hush fell over the room and all eyes turned to her as she marched to our row and sat two spots over. Her lackeys filed in after her and sat in silence. Celine glanced at me from under her thick lashes and gave me the kind of smile I'd imagine a poisonous snake might give its prey before striking.

"I can't believe they let that loser back here," Celina loudly to no one in particular.

A few of the people seated around her looked at her. Some nodded their heads in agreement, but it wasn't lost on me that a couple looked irritated or annoyed by Celine's presence. Interesting. I guess not everyone in this academy hated me for my unintended heroics.

"She better watch her back," Celine added.

"No one cares," Eva called over.

Celine leaned over the armrest next to her, her hair falling across her face in an obnoxious fashion. "No one was talking to *you*."

"The whole room could hear you," Eva snapped.

"Just drop it," I whispered out of the corner of my mouth, flushing red. I hated that more attention was falling on me now. What would have been a couple offhanded comments was turning into an argument that was far more interesting than waiting for Dean Bevan to appear and give us whatever words of wisdom he decided to impart.

I sunk down in my seat, trying to make myself less noticeable, and prayed that Eva would listen. Of course, my magic picked just that moment to manifest itself, coating my hands in smoky tendrils of shadow. A few murmurs and gasps went up around the room and I tried to pull the power back inside of me. I sucked a deep breath in through my nose and exhaled it through my mouth like instructor Glover had taught me. Slowly, bit by agonising bit, the shadows receded.

"Are you okay?" Eva sounded worried—for me, not about what I might do. I gave her a small nod.

"Fine. Just don't go challenging her, okay?"

"She was spouting bullshit!"

"I know, but I don't need to give her any more reason to hate me. She already blames me for her failed attempt to take over the academy and for the fact she's got a criminal record. I don't need her coming up with more ways to make my life unpleasant."

Beside me, Eva pouted, her lower lip protruding just slightly. "Sorry. I was just trying to defend my friend."

I didn't want her mad at me, too. "I know. I just... I need to be able to fight my own battles, that's all."

She nodded in understanding and turned so that she wasn't tempted to engage with Celine anymore. I did my best to avoid looking in her direction, too. My little loss of control was already more than I wanted her to see. If she knew how much she was getting to me, getting in my head, she'd be merciless. There was no way in hell I was going to let that happen.

Our little spat lost its intrigue as soon as Dean Bevan entered the room. Even from this distance I could see the dark circles under his eyes. His cheeks were paler and sunken. The summer clearly hadn't been kind to him, either. He approached the lectern and cleared his throat.

"Good afternoon, everyone. Welcome back." He wiped sweat from his brow with a dark cloth. "I know that for some of you, this summer has been life changing, and that for all of you, the last semester here at Braeseth wasn't without its challenges."

"Understatement of the year!" someone in the front of the room called out.

Dean Bevan cleared his throat again and raised his hands for silence. "I want to assure you all that you are safe here at Braeseth. We have had hex breakers in over the break and they have removed every last vestige of the curses laid on the academy."

"What about the druids?" someone else called out. "What happened to them?"

"The academy and the Council have come to the understanding that we can govern ourselves. Barring unexpected circumstances, we will not see druids on the grounds again. This year is a fresh start for all of us. I want you all to know that we value each and every one of you and your gifts. You are what makes this academy what it is. And together we are going to build each other up and make each other stronger."

Murmurs went up around the room, most doubting

his words. They were meant to be encouraging and positive, but we all knew they were hollow. Bevan was lucky to still be in power after everything that happened. The attack from the druid enforcers had happened under his nose, too. Sure, it wasn't as big of an embarrassment for him as for the Council, but I wouldn't be surprised if he'd faced a dressing down because of it.

"Now, I want you to put those events from your mind. Your studies will require your full commitment. As you are all aware: fail one class, and you'll be held back a year. Fail them all, and you will lose your position at the academy, and your magic will be bound."

A shiver ran through me despite myself. There was a time when that had seemed like the best thing in the world to me. I'd begged for it. But a lot had changed since then.

"Your gifts are a powerful responsibility," Bevan said, over the rising volume of discontented murmurs—the 'fail everything and get booted' rule was a new one from last year. "Prove that you are worth of them. I wish you all a good semester. Now if you'll excuse me, I need to prepare for the first years' arrival."

He hurried out of the room, leaving the rest of us to make our way up to the dorms. True to Glover's word, there were helpful little signs pointing us to the second-year dorms, and a list pinned to the main entrance with names and dorm numbers. I hung back, trying to blend in with the décor while Eva sought out our room assignment.

I clearly needed to work on my blending skills because I caught a few more glances coming my way as I waited. Unlike in the hall, these seemed less malicious and distrustful. Still, the moment they caught me staring back, they darted away or turned back to their friends.

"Looks like we got lucky. It's just you and me again," Eva said and tugged on my arm, leading us back through the cluster of students that still remained, and into the room on the far left. It was linked with one other room and shared a washroom. I pushed open the door to find our cases already set at the foot of each bed. The space had clearly been set up for only two occupants, so even though it was probably the same size as our room last year, it felt more spacious. I found a sheet of paper on my pillow listing classes for the coming semester. As Rathbone had said, Energy Manipulation was up first.

I settled back against the pillows and tried not to let my nerves get the better of me. Not everyone hated me, which could only be a good thing. But the fact I still couldn't control my magic threatened to put me in hot water with my instructors. As much as I wasn't a fan of classes, part of me didn't want to disappoint them. Of course, I also didn't want to drown them in shadow, and it seemed like my magic went from one extreme to the other.

If nothing else, this year was going to be interesting.

Chapter Three

I was the first one to the classroom the next morning. I'd snuck out and made my way to the canteen for a cup of coffee and some toast before Eva had roused herself. But now that meant I was standing there in the corridor alone, looking overeager. I'd slept badly last night thanks to my nerves getting the best of me. For all my big talk about wishing I was back at Braeseth, now that I was actually here, I was starting to wish I wasn't.

"You don't have to stand there alone," Instructor Rathbone said from inside the lecture room. I blinked in surprise. I hadn't even noticed him open the door.

"Oh, uh, thanks. I know I'm early," I mumbled into my shoulder and hoisted my bag onto my arm.

"Honestly, I'm not surprised to see you here ahead of the start time. I got the feeling you wanted a little privacy."

My head perked up at his words. Seriously, was he a telepath or something? "I just don't like people staring at me like I'm some weird loser."

"You aren't weird. And you're not a loser, either. What you did was very brave and selfless. I suspect many of your classmates are jealous of that bravery and don't know how else to express it."

"Well, they could just keep it to themselves," I said and set my bag at a desk in the back. There was one row of seats behind me but I doubted anyone would bother sitting there.

Slowly, other students filtered in. Eva settled beside me and I did my best to ignore the glares as other people tried to find seats away from us. Unfortunately, there were exactly enough desks for the number of students and a girl with a pixie cut was forced to take the desk right behind me. I noticed that Rory was sitting closer to me than he had all of last semester. Maybe our brief bonding over grades at the end of last year had stuck with him. When I caught his eye, he didn't stare at me like he wanted me dead, either. That was progress. That made exactly three people in this room who felt that way—two more than I'd expected.

At the front of the room, Instructor Rathbone clapped his hands together to draw the focus to him. "All right everyone, let's settle down. I know it's been a while since we've been together, so I am not expecting miracles today. But we are going to be testing to see how much you retained over the break. You're second years now, and that means the expectations are even higher. By the end of this semester, you should all be able to form sustained energy balls on command."

Clusters of excited whispers broke out throughout the

room—and not just from the guys. Seemed like everyone was excited to start slinging energy balls all around the place. Except me. We'd had to form an energy ball for our end-of-year exam last year, and we'd had an hour to pull it off. Doing it on command, which sort of suggested without taking a dozen attempts first, seemed like a stretch. But I'd been around Rathbone enough to know that he meant what he said. So if he expected us to do that, then there would be no argument. Either we'd pass or we'd fall flat on our faces.

"With that said, we're going to start with a warmup exercise today. You're going to be forming energy fields around both of your hands but not letting them extend beyond your wrists." He held up a hand to silence any arguments. "This will demonstrate how much control you have over your power."

"I can't believe I have to sit near her," Pixie Cut grumbled loud enough for me to hear.

"Get here earlier next time," the guy beside her said.

"I mean, she sided with the druids over us."

Don't react, Norah, I told myself, and firmly intended to follow my own advice. I didn't need to be getting into arguments in my first class. I would just keep my attention on Rathbone, and focus on getting the semester off to a good start. That was the smart thing to do.

Then again, I'd never been all that good at smart.

"For the record," I said, twisting round in my seat to glare at her, "I didn't side with the druids. I stopped them from stealing your magic. From stealing all of our magic."

"All right. Let's focus on the task at hand, shall we?" Rathbone's tone was firm and his message clear: he wouldn't put up with any other interruptions to his lesson. I wish he'd just let us have it out. I was getting sick of trying to take the high road and practically biting my own tongue off. Some people round here needed to be set straight on a few things, even if they didn't want to hear it. *Especially* if they didn't want to hear it.

The girl behind me let out an exaggerated huff but settled back in her chair. Instructor Rathbone took a seat behind his desk and clapped his hands together, signalling we should stop wasting time and start practicing. The room quieted as everyone turned their attention to their own magic. Even so, I could sense their gazes and attention lingering on me. Like they were assessing whether I was going to lose it on them. I tried to focus on my hands, to feel the ripple of electricity cascade over my skin but instead, tendrils of darkness wound their way around my fingers.

"Try to ignore them," Eva whispered, leaning across her desk.

"Easier said than done," I griped. "I don't know why they all think I'm some sort of monster. I didn't do anything to them." I balled my hands into fists, trying to quash the insecurity that seemed hell bent on calling up my shadow magic at the worst moments. My own irritation at everyone else only fed the shadows and they hardened against my skin, like armour trying to protect me.

"They don't hate you. At least not all of them," my friend assured me. There was a hitch in her breath and then she added, "Besides, I'm pretty sure you've got an admirer."

That was enough to pull my attention away from the shadows and I felt them recede, like some serpentine creature slithering back beneath the surface. "What admirer?"

Eva jutted her chin over her right shoulder, and I turned slowly, trying not to be obvious. At first, I didn't see anyone who I could call an admirer. Just a mix of classmates who were determined not to acknowledge I existed, and ones who were sending me painfully clear death stares. And then I spotted him. The guy from the market, only now he was wearing an academy uniform. I'd assumed he worked in one of the shops that day, and maybe he did, or maybe he'd been there for the same reasons I was. Getting his second year textbooks. He caught me looking and a touch of pink coloured his cheeks. He ducked his head before turning back to the task at hand.

"I don't even know him," I told Eva, lowering my voice and trying not to look his way again, which suddenly seemed like the hardest thing in the world.

"Well, he seems quite taken with you."

I glanced his way again, but he was staring at his hands, focusing on the thin layer of energy wrapped around them. I wished I could remember his name or even seeing him around campus last year. But nothing about him seemed familiar, other than from the market the other day. Then again, I'd spent last year much the same way as I planned to spend this year—avoiding everyone's attention, and keeping to myself. Which was going just great so far.

I just didn't get why he'd be interested in me. We'd only ever spoken that one time, as far as I could remember. And given how Celine had treated me last year, it was hard not to be suspicious. Being nice to anyone other than Eva had only ended with enemies and people hating me more.

I shook my head, pushing those thoughts aside. "I literally don't even know his name."

Eva rolled her eyes. "You're so bad at people. It's Reggie."

"Wait, how did you know that?"

"Because unlike some people," she teased, "I actually

pay attention to what's going on around me."

"Whatever. Let's just make it through this lesson and get out of here."

I focused on my hands, on the tiny cuticles that were rough and torn from normal wear and tear. There were little bits of skins stuck up at odd angles and I tried to imagine what they would feel like as electricity rippled across them, one at a time. Before my eyes, little rainbows of electrical current leapt from one torn bit of cuticle to the next, leaving behind an after image. I blinked but the colours remained. I'd never noticed how pretty the electricity we handled could be. Pressing my mouth into a firm line, I concentrated, trying to summon enough energy to let it spread up to my wrists.

"You're doing it," Eva whispered to me as I studied the rippling energy dancing around my hands.

I tried not to get too excited. I mean, this was supposed to be a basic magical skill. Everyone was meant to know how to do this by end of last year and I'd only barely succeeded then. I'd spent most of summer assuming that passing this class had been a fluke. But here I sat doing exactly what instructor Rathbone had asked us to do. And for longer than he'd instructed, too.

"Got lucky," I said and glanced her way.

She'd managed to get one hand to do what she wanted, but her right hand seemed to refuse to spark. I wondered whether I could jumpstart her with some of my energy. But that was probably cheating, and I knew my friend well enough to know she wouldn't want to manage it by breaking the rules. The moment of distraction was enough to disrupt my focus and the electricity which had until now been hovering neatly at my wrists zipped up to my elbows and decided to start spiralling outward in looping arcs. Panic fluttered in my throat and threatened to take hold for a moment before I managed to reign in the magic. The arcs tightened up again and bound themselves like bracelets to my arms.

"Ah! No, stop!"

The scream came from behind me and I blinked in confusion, panic thrumming through me again. The magic wrapped around my arms died and faded from existence as I twisted round, dreading what I would see.

The pixie haircut girl behind me was flailing about, trying to wave off bursts of electricity that didn't want to die. They were coming from her palms and raw, red blisters were forming on the backs of her hands and upper arms.

Instructor Rathbone was at her side in seconds, his hands glowing as he moved them over her extremities. I watched in awe as whatever magic he was using pulled the power from her and onto his own body. It crackled across his torso and made the ends of his hair stand on end from the charge. But he seemed unbothered by it and he had enough control over it to make it dissipate completely as he pulled it away from my classmate. How was he doing that? I stared at the energy, transfixed. It was like he was syphoning it off and then controlling it with his own magic.

Focus, Norah, focus. There was a girl right in front of me in absolute agony and all I could do was be impressed at Rathbone's control? A wave of nausea washed over me. I mean, sure, she'd been a bitch to me, but she was hardly the only one, and that didn't excuse my total lack of concern.

After a few tense moments, every last vestige of electrical energy was gone and all she had left were the blisters.

She winced as he probed them with the tip of one finger. "Get to the medical wing and have those treated."

"Is it going to scar?" she whimpered, tears sparkling in her eyes.

"No. You're going to be fine. But you'd better get going now." To the rest of the class he said, "Lesson's over."

She whimpered again and made a show of hissing as she picked up her bag and left the room. I watched as the rest of the class filed out. Several of them cast glances my way, and I tried not to react. I hadn't done anything to her. She'd lost control of her magic and that sucked, but it wasn't my fault. As he left, Reggie gave me another smile before he ducked his head and shuffled out of the room.

Since Rathbone had dismissed us partway through the lesson, we didn't have anywhere to be for another half hour. I didn't feel like leaving the classroom, and Eva seemed content to sit beside me. Rathbone gathered his things at the front of the room and left us in silence.

"I don't know why I thought this year was going to be any better than last year," I said with a heavy sigh, and buried my head in my hands.

"I'm telling you, not everyone was giving you dirty looks. And I'm sure as things get going and they have classes to worry about, they'll forgot about the drama with Celine."

"From your lips to their scrambled brains," I mumbled. "You know, this summer, I almost felt bad for Celine. She looked so scared during her trial and sentencing. Like she hadn't fully realised what was happening until it was hitting her."

"But she's the one who chose to break the rules and try to overthrow the dean. Not you. Actions have consequences, and she's old enough to know that."

"I know. And I know she deserved punishment." I picked at my fingernails. "But she's not wrong that because of what I did, her life is going to be different."

"You can't take responsibility for her. You can only worry about how your actions affect you," she said. "Just try to ignore them. It's going to die down. Besides, is it really worse than being at home?"

I snorted and looked over at her. "Honestly, I don't know. At home, I could hide in my room and so long as I didn't come out, no-one would bother me. But here, I have to be seen. I have to interact. If I had my way, no one would notice me."

"Did your parents really make it that uncomfortable over break?"

"They watched me every second they could with this haunted look in their eyes. Like I was going to explode at any moment. I spent so long wanting to be noticed, but as soon as I was, I kinda wished I was back in Micah's shadow. And it's such a double standard. They are so devoted to him, even though what he did was wrong. And I didn't do anything wrong, but they look at me like I'm the dangerous one."

"Well, they aren't here now," she said and patted me on the shoulder.

It wasn't much of a comfort. Even if I didn't have to worry about my parents judging me, I still had to worry about the rest of the academy. Eva might have believed in me, but she was the only one. How the hell was I supposed to convince an academy full of bored students that I wasn't anyone special or important enough to bother hating?

Chapter Four

By some small miracle, the rest of the day passed without anyone setting themselves on fire, and the whispering behind my back wasn't nearly as obvious. I even caught a few people eying me with what could only be described as smiles on their faces.

"When do you think they'll teach us how to make ourselves invisible?" I groaned to Eva as we trudged out of botany shortly before five o'clock that evening. Having barely passed last year, I was already fighting to catch up on day one.

"Can't you already do that with your shadows?" she said, raising an eyebrow. I shrugged.

"I did that one time, and I haven't got the first idea how." I switched my bag to the other shoulder and sighed dreamily. "I mean, like proper invisibility."

She just shook her head at me and laughed. "It'll all die down in a few days. Let everyone get their curiosity out of their systems and then they'll go back to pretending you don't exist, and you won't be at risk of having a heart attack."

I didn't have a witty comeback to her as we stood in line to get food. Somehow we'd beaten most of our year down here and I didn't see many new faces. I'd expected that some of the third years would be getting food in before they went off to do whatever it was they did but they, too, were absent. That was weird. Unease gnawed at the edge of my consciousness.

By the time the kitchen mage had filled my plate and I'd grabbed a mug of coffee, that unease was turning the contents of my stomach to acid and the food that looked so appetising moments ago was threatening to make me retch. I slid into a seat and Eva sat opposite me with her equally unappetising food.

"I'm telling you," she pressed on, "it's all going to blow over. In a few days, everyone will be so consumed with classes they won't remember what you've done or haven't done."

"Can't come soon enough," I grumbled, pushing food around my plate in a pathetic attempt to look like I was eating. The kitchen mages were one of the best things about Braeseth, but even their miracles couldn't tempt me right now.

"Norah, listen to me. You can't spiral. First off, not eating due to stress is clearly *my* thing," she said. Her tone was sharp, commanding, and it made me look up. The expression on her face told me she was barely keeping in the laughter that made her eyes crinkle at the edges. She got serious. "And I will not have my best friend suffering from crippling self-doubt. You did what you did and if they can't handle it, that's their problem, not yours."

"Weird pep talk, Eva, but thanks," I replied, and forced a smile.

She turned back to her food and I did the same, praying it didn't make a repeat appearance. I made it through a couple of bites when I felt the tiny hairs on the nape of my neck stand on end. They bristled like I was being watched. I wasn't exactly known for my subtlety, but I took a breath and made myself turn ever-so-slowly to look over my shoulder. A girl with a shock of purple-pink hair that fell across one side of her face at an angle eyed me with such intensity I was surprised her gaze hadn't bored holes into my skull.

She looked down when she realised I'd caught her ogling me and I thought I saw a touch of pink on her cheeks. At least she had the decency to feel embarrassed. I snorted and turned back to my food.

"So," Eva said with a whole lot of forced levity. "What did you think of our first day back?"

"Well, I suppose it wasn't a total disaster," I said begrudgingly. "Botany's going to be rough again. I don't know why. Plants shouldn't be that hard to understand. I managed to electrocute one this afternoon. I was only trying to repot it. So I tried giving it some water, and, well, I'm pretty sure it's not going to make it through the night. Bloody suicidal vegetation."

She snickered. "You just have to know how to listen to them. It's a lot more like science than magic."

"I was never much good with that, either." I stopped prodding at my food and took a long swig from my mug of cooling coffee.

"Well, we've got unique magics tomorrow morning, so I'm sure that will take your mind off sucking at botany."

"That one's bound to be a barrel of laughs. You know, I'm pretty sure I heard a couple of guys taking bets on whether my shadow magic would try to kill someone."

"Well, I suppose a better question would be whether you get to choose who it attempts to kill. Because I have some suggestions…"

I smirked. "Oh, and we've got that new runes class."

She cocked her head to the side. "Don't think I saw that one on my timetable."

I rummaged through my bag and pulled out the list of courses I'd found on my bed. I handed it over, tapping the block right after unique magics. "See."

She pulled out her own page and compared them. "Looks like you got an extra class that I didn't. Wonder how that happened?" She set the pages down and tried to cover her mouth with both hands. "Sorry, that was totally horrible. I didn't mean it like that. Of course you should be in classes I'm not."

I waved away her concern. "Relax, it's fine. And I don't know, I remember last year instructor Rathbone telling me he thought I'd do well in his Runes class. I guess he decided to sign me up." Without asking me first. I'm sure his *intentions* were good, at least.

"Well, you'll have to tell me how it is. I've got advanced botany then."

Which I was a whole lot of happy I didn't have to take. The little hairs on my neck bristled again and I turned to see the girl with the swooping hair eying me again. This time she'd gotten out of her seat and was shifting from foot to foot, like she couldn't decide whether to approach or run the other way.

"Norah, don't do anything stupid," Eva said, catching the direction of my stare.

By the time she'd finished speaking I was already out of my seat, stalking over to the girl. I didn't recognise her, so she must have been a first year—one who never learned that it was rude to stare. She blinked up at me through her curtain of hair and this close I could see her eyes were a dazzling shade of cobalt blue that created a stark contrast to her hair. Yeah, she definitely looked like she belonged at a school for the rejects of the magical community. She'd fit right in here at Misfits. She certainly seemed to have the right bitchy attitude.

She clearly didn't expect me to approach because she

took a step forward and nearly collided with me.

"Whatever you have to say, just say it," I snapped. "No need to hide and lurk about. Just spit it out." My voice reverberated around the canteen, and I felt as much as saw several sets of eyes turn our way, but frankly, I was past caring.

"S-sorry," she stammered, casting her vibrant gaze toward her shoes.

"No." I shook my head, slashing my hair through the air. "I'm tired of everyone walking around saying things behind my back. You've clearly got an opinion, so let's have it."

She cleared her throat and brushed her hair out of her face so she could look at me. "I just wanted to tell you... I think you were really brave."

Her words hit me like a fist, rattling my skull and taking far too long for my brain to process what my ears just heard. "What?"

"I wasn't here last year, but we heard about what you did. You saved the academy. You could have just let it happen or run away and let someone else fix the problem. But you didn't. You fought back, and you protected people, people you didn't know. People who didn't like you because they're just bigots. But you saved them all the same."

Without warning, she threw her arms around me in a

tight embrace. "You're a hero, and I just wanted to tell you that we believe in you. And we're grateful for what you did. You made sure we had a place to come and learn magic that was safe."

I stood there in the middle of the canteen with this strange girl wrapped around me, giving me praise, and I wanted to crawl out of my skin. I wasn't used to people telling me that I was a hero or a role model. Sure, it was better than being called a traitor or worse by Celine and her ilk, but it still felt...wrong. Unnatural. I never wanted to be a hero. I just knew I couldn't let Celine or the druids destroy the academy. As much as I'd wanted my powers gone, this place had started to feel like home and a place worth protecting.

I patted the girl's back a time or two and I tried to pull free without making it seem like I really didn't want physical interaction. She took the hint and let go, stepping back. "Sorry, I get kind of emotional meeting important people."

"How'd you even know about what happened if this is your first year?" I said, still not quite sure she had the right person. Brave? Important? That didn't sound like me.

"My older sister graduated last year. She heard about what happened and gushed about it all summer. I think she wanted me to know that it was okay for me to come.

And she wanted to tell you thank you for saving her, too."

"Honestly, I never spent much time with the third years," I said.

"Oh, I don't think you ever met her. But she knew who you were. She said that you made her proud to graduate from Braeseth."

"Oh, well, uh, thanks I guess."

"And you make me proud to be here, too," she added and reached out to offer her hand. "I'm Belinda, by the way. Belinda Croft."

I caught the glint in those brilliant irises, like she hoped even just a little that the last name might mean something to me. It didn't, and I was surprised how much I suddenly wished it did. But I wasn't sure I could even name half the students in my own year. I took her proffered hand and gave it a firm shake.

"Nice to meet you, Belinda Croft. Do me a favour, though, and next time you want to talk to me, just come over."

She grinned. "Totally." After a beat, she added, "Bye."

I watched her retreat to her table, and I did the same. Eva sat with her mug covering her face, which did nothing to hide the amused smile on her lips. "You've got a fan girl."

"Shut up," I grumbled, and swirled the contents of my mug around.

"It's cute." She grinned and elbowed me. "Oh, come on, you can't possibly be pissed that someone has your back and believes in what you did."

"Can we talk about something else?" I begged, feeling the beginnings of a red flush working their way up my neck. "Anything else? Please?"

She shrugged and leaned forward, elbows propped on the edge of the table. "Are you going to try and reach out to Zachary? I think as second years we have more freedom to leave the grounds on weekends."

I guess I should have been a little more specific with the 'anything'. I really should know by now that Eva did not need that much leeway. Ever. Ah, well, I brought that one on myself.

"If he's interested in seeing me, he can reach out," I said, drumming my fingers on the side of the mug.

I'd spent more nights this summer than I cared to count holding that communication stone from Kelsey and trying to find a way to contact him—not that I was about to admit it. I'd almost reached out to Kelsey herself to see if she knew a way to get in touch, but it seemed dumb to bother her with something so trivial. We were friends, sort of, but I'd be using her position at the Council for romantic aims and that just felt wrong.

"You two were pretty cute at the Valentine's dance," Eva said with a snicker.

"I'm not denying he's attractive. I kissed him, didn't I? But he made it perfectly clear that while he was here, nothing could happen. And honestly, why's he going to bother with me, anyway? I'm still in training. He's got a career. He's probably forgotten about me."

"Girl, he most certainly has not forgotten about you."

I rolled my eyes. "Did you miss the part where he avoided me a good three months after I kissed him? Trust me, he's *really* good at avoidance."

"You could try to reach out to him. You do recall that you're living in the twenty-first century, right? It's not a crime for the woman to call first. You are absolutely not over him, and you deserve to be happy. Besides, he knows all your history. He's not going to judge you for it. He proved that already."

"But won't that look like I'm chasing him?"

"Sometimes people need to be chased."

"Even if I wanted to, I don't have a way to get in touch," I said, which wasn't strictly true. I had a way… I just wasn't quite sure how to use it. Or why.

"We both know that's a pathetic excuse. Don't make me twist your arm. Find a way to reach out. Like I said, you deserve to be happy."

She made her face into a stern glare, and it was all I

could do not to burst out laughing. I settled for rolling my eyes.

"Okay, fine. I'll try."

"Good, because one of us needs some romance."

I slid a hand into the bottom of my bag where the communication stone had sat since the last time I'd used it. I should just bite the bullet and contact Kelsey. I didn't even know Zachary's last name, and I'd wager there were more than a few who might have stones like these. And I still barely knew how to use the stupid thing. For all I knew, it might actually only connect me to Kelsey, anyway.

Rathbone might know.

He had seen me using it last year. Still, it felt awkward asking an instructor for help reaching out to my crush. I shuddered at the thought. I didn't much fancy explaining that one. *Please, Instructor, can you help me use this stone to call the handsome druid I'm in lo—* No. I definitely was not *that*. I just liked him, that was all.

The doors to the canteen opened and a rush of people came in. I didn't see Celine or her cronies, but that didn't mean they weren't on their way. I had no desire to share the same space with them any more than I had to for lessons. Not wanting to be subject to their stares and whispers—even if some of them were supportive—I cleared my plate and mug and started for the dorms. Eva caught up to me halfway to the second floor.

"Hey, you know I wasn't trying to annoy you," she said, her twists falling against her right shoulder as she walked.

"No, I know. It wasn't that. I just... I can't deal with all those people right now. I know some of them mean well. But I don't want groupies or fans. I just want to be left alone. I want to learn how to control my magic so I don't fail at the end of the year."

"Okay. Good. I just didn't want you to be mad at me."

I wrapped an arm around her shoulders and gave her a light squeeze. "Never. After all, I need my wing woman. As I recall, I wouldn't have looked nearly as good as I did during that dance without your expert fashion sense."

She knitted her eyebrows and shuddered at the memory.

"I've never met anyone with such a lack of style. It's a good thing we have to wear uniforms."

"My pride is wounded," I feigned, clutching a hand over my heart.

She giggled as we walked side by side for a few paces. Then she stopped suddenly and I lurched forward, my arm flying awkwardly over her head so I didn't accidentally brain her.

"Well, you'll have to do your romancing without me,"

she said. "I just remembered I need to check some books out of the library for something I promised my mum I would look up. I'll see you back at the room later, okay?"

She scurried off before I could even finish muttering a, "See you," and I frowned after her vanishing back. Her explanation was oddly vague by her standards. Was Eva lying to me? Maybe she had a secret guy she was embarrassed to tell me about. A smile tugged at the corners of my mouth. I hoped so. For one thing, if she hooked up with someone, she might stop trying to fix my love life... because some things were just doomed.

I stood there in the corridor for a long moment trying to reach a decision. I could just go back to the dorm and reach out to Kelsey, hoping she responded, or I could go look for Instructor Rathbone and pick his brain on how the bloody stone actually worked and if I could find a way to reach out to Zachary. I'd have thought all these months without seeing each other would have dulled the image of him in my mind, but it was still crisp. Still handsome and still perfect—and still infuriating that he'd basically ghosted me.

There was a third option. I could just go back to the dorm and ignore the problem. Except my roommate was a living lie detector and she'd sniff out the lie as soon as it left my mouth. I pivoted toward the dorm anyway, because when it came down to it, asking Kelsey was bound to be less embarrassing than asking Rathbone, and unlike him, she was actually likely to know Zachary's last name—or at least be able to find out.

I made it halfway down the corridor when footsteps rang out behind me, and then a sting of electricity zapped my back, sending me stumbling into the nearest wall.

Chapter Five

My back tingled as the energy dissipated. I braced myself against the wall in front of me, giving myself a moment to catch my breath. I didn't need to look behind me to know who was on the other end of that energy blast. Slowly, I pivoted to find Celine and her friends glowering at me. Celine held out her hands and the icy blue tendrils of her electricity crackled around her fingertips. She wasn't even bothering to hide that she'd attacked me. Students had been expelled for less, and that would mean her powers being bound, but she didn't seem to care. Either she'd really lost it, or she knew me well enough to know I wouldn't rat on her without good reason. Maybe both.

Her glower twisted into a sneer and the energy leapt off her skin and wrapped around my wrists. She tried to yank me forward but I dug in my heels and resisted, pulling back as hard as I could. Some part of my brain registered that I should be feeling my skin blistering and burning under the assault, but there was nothing. I risked a glance down. A thin layer of shadow wrapped around my hands and arms up to the elbows, protecting me like armour. I hadn't even consciously called the shadows. Maybe it was just a defence mechanism. I lifted my head to make eye contact with Celine.

"You know it's against academy rules to use your powers on another student," I said calmly, my voice not betraying my hammering heart. The tug of war between her and my wrists continued, and the energy grew brighter, thicker.

Celine shrugged one shoulder, sending her fiery red hair cascading down her back. "And what makes you think I give a damn about academy rules?"

Fair point. Given that she'd tried to overthrow the dean last year, it was pretty clear she didn't care much about breaking the rules. I'd have thought her time in prison would have been enough to instil a healthy respect for the law, but maybe I was giving her more credit than she deserved.

I stood my ground and forced myself not to react— the other two hadn't attacked me yet, and if she wanted to do me serious harm, she'd have done it while my back was turned.

Celine's lips pressed together in a thin line and she released my wrists, apparently realising she wasn't going to get anywhere that way, and the energy receded and disappeared back into her fingertips. The shadows on my arms stayed in place.

"What do you want, Celine?" I asked, leaning against the wall. I didn't want to let her see that her little zap had caught me more off guard than I'd realised. My back muscles and arms were starting to spasm from the shock, and I could feel a deep throbbing pain spreading through my muscles.

"To finish our conversation from the market. Before we were so rudely interrupted," she answered, plastering a fake smile on her lips. She looked like a shark coming in for the kill.

"Look, I'm sorry you got punished, but you deserved it," I replied.

She stepped up so we were toe-to-toe and leaned in close. "Deserved it?" she snarled. "I was trying to change the world. For the better. And they celebrate you for stopping it. That's what's wrong with this place. They reward cowardice!"

I shook my head and worked hard to keep the frustration from my voice—and probably failed. "When will you get it? I don't want people to notice me. I don't want to be famous or in the spotlight. I just want to live my life."

"Well, at least you get to live your life how you want," Miranda said.

"What's that supposed to mean?" My forehead furrowed as I searched her face.

Celine let out a harsh bark of laughter. "You can't really be that stupid, can you, Norah? You know what you did to us."

"I bargained for a lighter sentence," I said. "They didn't want to even let you come back. You know that, right?"

"Because of you, we went to prison." Celine's entire body shivered on the last word, and I didn't get the sense she was faking it. I'd been to visit my brother in a prison holding facility once, and I'd seen the effect the place had on him. But that had been maximum security, for terrorists and murderers. Celine had been sent to minimum security—I'd heard the sentence. It couldn't have been nearly as bad, could it? Still, I watched Celine rub at her wrists, and I could almost see the faint indentations of something circular. Like cuffs. Had they been made to wear magic suppressing cuffs the whole time?

My stomach did a flip at that possibility. I hated those things. They made anyone who wore them look so much less than they were. It diminished not only their magic but their spirit. But I wasn't the one who'd broken the law, and she'd known her actions would have consequences.

"I won't apologise for that," I said.

"Because of you, we can't get jobs. We'll always be criminals. Less than we already are because we had to come through this place," Celine said. Her eyes went unfocused and even though she stood there in front of me, it was clear her mind had transported her somewhere else.

"I'm sure there are loads of jobs for you out there," I said, hoping to assuage her.

"No. There will never be a job worthy of me out there now," she said, and her gaze focused in on me again. "Do you have any idea what it was like in there?"

"No. I don't." I felt anger welling in my gut. I'd had enough of listening to her acting like her sentence—the one she'd *earned*—was undeserved and horrific. "But I know it was nothing like what my brother has had to face. You should count yourself lucky."

She slammed a fist into my jaw and pain exploded across my face. My head cracked against the wall behind me and black dots spotted my vision. I blinked hard, trying to clear the dots and the dizziness, neither with much success.

Celine was still glaring at me. She lowered her hand, but the fist remained clenched tight at her side.

"The guards treated us like dirt. Made fun of us for being there. They knew what we'd tried to do. They called us terrorists. Said we deserved worse than we got." Her voice quivered with a level of fear I'd never heard in her voice. Not even when we'd been facing down Seneca.

I wanted to tell her that all prison guards were arseholes like that, but I knew that would only piss her off more. Making her more unstable was the opposite of what I needed to do if I wanted to walk away mostly intact.

"That's awful," I said, not meeting her gaze.

"For the first few weeks, anyway." Her tone changed, taking on a tougher quality. "It was pretty clear we had the respect of the other prisoners."

"No one messed with us," Miranda said, her eyes glinting with a cold pride.

Celine threw her head back and laughed, mouth open, body shaking. As scared as I might have been when she'd attacked me out of nowhere, that sort of unhinged behaviour sent a new wave of chills through my body. I hadn't taken into account just how much being locked up would affect her mental state. Yet another miscalculation in my attempt to quell a brewing fight between the Council and the rest of us.

"You'd be surprised what people in a minimum-security facility can teach you in six weeks," Celine whispered, leaning in so close our bodies touched. "The kind of pain you can inflict without leaving marks. The ways you can warp a person's mind."

I turned my head to the side so I didn't have to look at her. I didn't want her to see the terror etching itself on my face. The way her voice dropped an octave as she spoke only amped up the promise of pain she was offering. Her breath was hot against my cheek as I stood there, pinned between her weight and the wall.

"What is going on here?" Instructor Rathbone's voice echoed down the hall.

"This isn't over. You won't always have people rushing in to save you," Celine hissed in my ear before she stepped away.

I was grateful that the wall was there to keep me upright as she retreated to join her cronies. Instructor Rathbone came into view, striding down the hallway towards us.

"Nothing," Celine answered him, arms crossed over her chest. "Just catching up after summer break."

Rathbone eyed me. He clearly didn't believe that—for all Celine's newfound skills, it was clear lying wasn't amongst them. But right now, I wasn't sure antagonising her by telling Rathbone what had happened was a smart move. There was something not right about Celine, and I didn't need to give her another excuse to go after me.

"Norah?" Rathbone probed. "Are you all right?" The concern in his eyes overwhelmed me and I swallowed hard, then ducked his eye.

"Really, it's fine," I said.

Rathbone pivoted to face the other girls. "Get back to your dorms, now."

"Whatever," Celine huffed and stalked down the hall,

her friends in tow.

I exhaled heavily. Without the threat of more pain, my legs shook, and my knees gave way. I didn't stop myself from sliding to the floor. At least I was strong enough not to burst into tears in front of an instructor.

Rathbone was silent a moment, then sat on the floor beside me.

"I need you to be honest with me, Norah. Are you okay? Did they hurt you?"

"Nothing worse than a mistake in class would have done," I said, balling my hands into fists to keep my emotions in check.

"What provoked her?"

I couldn't help but laugh. "I exist? I don't know. I was heading back to the dorms and all of a sudden she just jumped me. I didn't do anything to her."

"You need to be careful. Especially around her."

Obviously.

"I know. And I didn't break any rules."

He fixed me with an understanding smile. "You know, if she attacked you, using your magic in self-defence wouldn't be considered breaking the rules."

"Right," I murmured, studying the cracks in the floor between my feet.

"I can talk to her," he offered.

"What?" I swallowed my panic and tried to make my

voice calm. "No. Don't do that."

"What she's doing isn't just against academy rules, Norah. It's assault."

"She's just mad at me, that's all. She'll get over it. Trust me, if you get involved, it will just make things worse."

"I know the end of last year was rough for you, and this can't be easy, coming back here where it all happened," he said, and I could hear the sincerity in his voice. "If you need someone to talk to, I'm around."

I couldn't look at him. It felt strange having him offer his support like that. Especially when his words conjured a different face that I wanted to confide in. If he'd been here, Zachary would have understood what I was feeling. I would have actually told him how bloody terrified I'd been when Celine had come at me. How I still felt so damned defenceless and useless with my magic. If I told Rathbone those fears, he would... What? He knew it was a struggle for me. He'd taught me all last year. But I didn't want his judgment or his effort to fix me.

But maybe he could give me a way to get what I needed after all. Asking for his help with the communication stone hadn't been my first choice but since he was here, it was worth a shot.

"Do we need to make a stop at the infirmary?" Rathbone's voice was soft, like he knew he was intruding on my inner thoughts and was trying to be polite.

"Stop? What?" Maybe Celine's magic had scrambled my brain in addition to my muscles.

"I ran into your roommate and she told me you were heading this way. I was actually looking for you. But if you think you need to be seen at the infirmary first, then let's go."

He took me by the elbow and guided me to my feet. I was about to protest but my back spasmed and stole my breath away.

"That might be a good idea," I admitted as I tried to fill my air with lungs. My legs were still wobbly, and I couldn't stand up straight. Her magic had never caused this kind of damage before.

Instructor Rathbone ushered me forward, one hand secure around my shoulders to make sure I didn't fall. I hadn't realised he grabbed my bag until we were in the infirmary and I sat on a bed. He pulled the curtain around us, and we waited for one of the healers to approach.

"How are you doing?"

I tried to take a deeper breath and found it wasn't as jarring as it had been in the corridor.

"I think it's easing now," I said. I tried to straighten up, but that just made the pain worse and I failed to hide the grimace on my face. So much for that.

He gave me a sympathetic look. "What did she do,

exactly?"

Did he know something I didn't?

"Just hit me with some electricity," I said.

"Her specialty," he muttered as the curtain slid to one side and a woman with rosy cheeks and a long, pointed nose appeared. She had her hair wound in a knot at the top of her head. I could spot intricate little twists like Eva wore leading up the knot. It was enough to temporarily distract me from the pain.

"So, Ms Sheehan, I hear you're having some magic-induced muscle spasms?"

"Guess so. Never felt anything like this before," I said, and tried to give her a smile that didn't convey the pain still dancing down my spine.

She turned to Rathbone and made a little shooing motion. "I'm going to need to apply a little topical cream to the affected area. It should take only a few minutes to work. But it will require privacy."

"Right, of course." Rathbone stepped beyond the curtain and turned so his silhouette was very clearly facing the other way. I tugged my top up to my neck and let out an audible hiss as the cold cream hit my skin.

"Wait a minute or two before pulling down your top and you'll be fine. The pain should stop immediately but I would avoid any strenuous physical activity for a few days. These types of injuries have a way of popping back up if the muscles are overworked."

"Got it," I sighed and waited for the cream to do its job. It wasn't like I had plans to do anything strenuous tomorrow. Or ever.

True to her word, it only took another two minutes before my back had a nice numb feeling. I pressed the tips of my fingers to the spot that had hurt worst and was pleased to not feel anything beyond the slight pressure of my fingers on my skin. I pulled down my top and stepped around the curtain to find instructor Rathbone standing sentry. It was almost sweet, if a bit overbearing.

"I think I can make it back to my dorm by myself," I said and stepped up beside him. I didn't need everyone else thinking I couldn't go anywhere without a bodyguard.

"You aren't going back to your dorm, Norah," he said. "Not yet, anyway."

He paused to hold the door open for me.

"I'm not?" I trailed him into the corridor. Wait, he said he'd been looking for me in the first place. That was... odd. "Wait, you said you talked to Eva. Why were you coming to find me?"

"Dean Bevan needs to see you in his office."

Chapter Six

I stopped walking as soon as he mentioned Bevan's name. As much as I didn't want Rathbone swooping in as my protector, I hated him acting as the dean's messenger even more. The fact he'd already been looking for me when I got jumped by Celine meant Bevan couldn't possibly be on my case about that. Which meant he'd heard about what happened in energy manipulation this morning.

"I haven't done anything," I protested, crossing my arms over my chest.

Rathbone looked at me over his shoulder and gave me a smile. "Just come along, would you?"

I wanted to throw a fit and tell him I wasn't going anywhere near the dean's office when whatever he wanted to chastise me for wasn't even my fault. But I was also not a bloody toddler and wouldn't be winning any favour by acting like one. So I gave the biggest eye roll I could muster and trudged after him.

We descended to the first floor and as we passed by the open front doors in the entry hall, wind ruffled the hem of my shirt, tickling the dulled sensation in my back. I paused, letting the cool air soothe my skin before Rathbone made a "hurry up" gestured and I fell back into step with him. The closer I got to Bevan's office, the more flashes disrupted my vision. Memories of last year. Of what Celine and her friends had wanted to do. What they'd wanted *me* to do. Phantom versions of them danced in my vision and I watched them dart into the office and incapacitate the dean. He sat there in his chair, unmoving. Unconscious.

Rathbone held the door open for me and gave me something that was halfway between a pat and a shove between the shoulder blades, leaving me no choice but to enter the room. Bevan was awake and alert, watching me from behind his desk. My eye was drawn to the sphere sitting on the shelf behind his desk. Unlike last time I'd been here, it had an added sheen that I guessed was some sort of protective magic to keep students from messing with the wards around the academy.

"Thank you for coming down, Ms Sheehan," Bevan said, and gestured to the chair across from him. "Please have a seat."

I glanced over my shoulder at Rathbone, but he didn't respond. He just stood there like a sentry, blocking my exit. Traitor. I dipped my head in the smallest of nods, and perched on the edge of the chair, hands balled into fists. I concentrated on the feeling of my nails leaving indentations in the flesh of my palms. If I had something to distract me, something else to focus on, maybe I'd be less likely to lose it when he blamed me for that girl's injuries in class.

"Look, I didn't do anything to that girl in class." I was speaking to Bevan, but I looked over my shoulder to Rathbone. "I didn't touch her. I know my magic got a little out of control, but I didn't hit her. It wasn't me."

"Instructor Rathbone, what is she talking about?" Bevan asked, sounding genuinely perplexed.

"Nothing important, Dean Bevan," Rathbone replied.

My confusion muddled my ability to speak. If Bevan didn't know about what happened in class, then why send Rathbone to drag me back here?

"You… You're not mad about…" I blinked at my instructor, and he shook his head.

"I know that wasn't your fault, Norah."

Relief flooded my body, releasing the built-up tension in the muscles along my neck and shoulders. I winced as they loosened, the effect cascading down my back. Apparently tensing in anticipation of punishment was akin to strenuous physical activity because my back started to flare again. I uncurled my fingers only to clamp them down on the arms of the chair.

"Then why am I here?" I managed.

Bevan smiled at me across his desk. "To discuss your future."

"Uh, what?"

"It's a discussion I would have liked to have at the end of last year but well, given everything that happened, it was deemed best to wait."

"So this is like, what, career counselling?"

"Of a sort, I suppose." He paused and shuffled through papers in front of him. "Do you have any plans for after graduation?"

"That's still two years away," I answered. *And I'm not entirely convinced I'll make it to graduation.*

"Surely you've thought about what you'd like to do with your life once you have finished your studies here at Braeseth?" He raised an eyebrow at me.

That Valentine's Day conversation with Zachary popped into my head. That little bookstore café with the druid enforcer turned bookseller recommending reading material while I sold coffee was a pretty dream. But it wasn't a viable reality. And envisioning the two of us together like that only made me realise how much I'd been burying the hurt at his absence. Why did guys have to be so damned annoying? The fact was, he'd already chosen his career, and he'd worked damned hard to get there. Even if I didn't like what he did for a living, I had to acknowledge he was good at it. He *did* good. And me, I still didn't know what I wanted to do in the real world. I wasn't that good at anything.

"No, I haven't," I answered eventually.

"Nothing at all?" Bevan prompted.

"Nope." But I was starting to get the sense he had a suggestion.

"Perhaps you might like to consider a career in law enforcement?"

He isn't serious. Never in a million years would that have been a possibility. Not in the most childhood fuelled fantasy world would I have ever dreamed of being a law enforcement officer. For one thing, I'd never been inclined toward enforcing anything. The serious look on Bevan's face only made the absurdity of his statement clearer, and I burst into laughter. Bending double, I peeled my hands off the arms of the chair to clutch at my stomach.

"That's really funny," I managed between gasps for air.

"It wasn't a joke," Bevan said, sounding mildly irked. I took in the droop of his lips and his quivering chin, and tried to compose myself.

"Law enforcement, like… an enforcer? Me?" The words sounded so foreign coming out of my mouth.

"I don't see why it is so farfetched, Ms Sheehan. You showed immense bravery defending the academy last year. You clearly know right from wrong and are willing to fight for it."

"Yeah, but that doesn't mean I'd be good at that kind

of job," I said.

"I know that you had a difficult time last year adjusting to life here. And having your unique magic manifest so late complicated matters, of course, but you really should be proud of how far you've come. You shouldn't be so self-deprecating."

He was just trying to motivate me, I was sure, but as compliments went, it was kind of a backhanded one. I didn't like other people telling me how I should feel about my own situation. I had enough issues handling it myself.

"Yeah, well, it's not like it's an option," I said, shaking my head. I couldn't believe we were even having this conversation.

"And why not?"

I snorted. "Look around you. We aren't at the druid academy. And last time I checked, only druids can become druid enforcers. It's kind of in the name."

"There is a first time for everything," Bevan murmured and turned his attention back to the papers on his desk. Whatever he'd been looking for earlier, he hadn't found it. Or maybe he'd forgotten.

"Excuse me?"

He held up one of the pages with a triumphant expression and passed it over to me. "Yes, here we are. I received this from the enforcer academy. It seems someone there took notice of what you've done and is very interested in you."

An itchy, crawling sensation prickled at my skin. Druids were interested in me? I was having a hard time imagining any way that could be a good thing. It had been druid enforcers who'd locked up my brother. Good or bad, they'd been harsher on him than necessary.

Still, I took the letter he brandished at me and skimmed the contents. It was an invite to participate in some classes at the Krakenvale Academy of Druidic Law Enforcement, which sounded very grand—and utterly ridiculous. I mean, it was right there in the name: *Druidic*. There was nothing even remotely druidic about me.

"I don't understand," I said and laid the paper down on my lap.

"Well, as I said, they were impressed by your actions last year and wanted to offer you a chance to study there. Not fulltime, mind you, but for a few weeks. It would be a great opportunity for you. And Instructor Rathbone tells me you're doing wonderfully in his class." Bevan raised his gaze over my shoulder to Rathbone, and I caught the instructor's nod from the corner of my eye.

So that was why Rathbone had been involved. I was surprised Instructor Glover wasn't here cheering me on, too. Then again, she was more of a realist. She wouldn't say something just to stroke my ego. I hadn't thought

Rathbone would either.

"That's not how it works," I said bluntly.

"But it could be." Bevan leaned forward, his eyes boring into mine, as if by the intensity of his gaze he could convince me that this was the best idea in the world.

"They want me to what… be some sort of test case?" I snapped.

"Think of the possibilities. You could be paving the way for real reform in our justice system, Norah." Bevan was practically gushing, and his sudden lack of formality as he addressed me amped up my discomfort.

"No. Not interested," I answered, tossing the paper back across the desk.

"It's not something you'd have to decide right now, but they will need an answer before Halloween," Bevan said, as though I hadn't just given it to him.

"Like I said, I'm not interested in whatever they're offering. I did what I did because it was the right thing to do, but that doesn't mean I like or trust druids. They're part of the reason my family is so messed up."

"Your brother's actions spoke for themselves," Rathbone said quietly from the doorway.

"And the way the system treated him was atrocious. Stripping his magic when he was only a small part of the problem. And I know it wasn't the enforcers who sentenced him, but they're the ones who dragged him away. They're part of what's broken."

Because resent and hate Micah or not for what he did, he was still my brother. And the less I had to do with the system that destroyed him, the better.

Bevan gestured at me. "And that is exactly why you should consider their offer. You could be the change you want to see in the world. You could make certain others aren't treated the way he was."

"I'm not going to be some experiment," I spat. "I can't believe they can't see how that sounds."

"But it's a good thing," Bevan tried.

"No, it's not. They're doing this because they know that things between us and them are still tense. They want to trot me out like some prize pig, to say 'See, we're progressive. We're teaching one of them'. That mentality is exactly what led to problems in the first place."

It had been the tiny nugget of Celine's plan that had actually resonated with me last year, and though I'd turned away from it eventually, there were parts of the doubt that remained. We weren't less than them, and until they saw that, we *couldn't* co-exist.

"Please, Ms Sheehan. Reconsider."

"No. I don't want anything from them. Tell them no. I don't know what I want to do with my life, but I know it's not that."

I stood and pivoted to face Rathbone. Instead of stopping me, he stepped aside and let me leave. I didn't stop to listen as Bevan protested my leaving without being dismissed. I stayed on high alert the whole way back to the dorms. Between Celine's attack and Bevan's pushy 'offer', I was wound more than a little tight.

"Where've you been?" Eva asked when I trudged into the room, easing the door shut behind me.

"Through hell?" I said, and flopped onto my bed.

She set her book down and moved to sit on the edge of the bed beside me. "What's going on? Talk to me. Is it Zachary?"

I let out a strained laugh. "I didn't even get to try reaching out. I was on my way back here to contact a friend who might know how to get in touch when Celine jumped me. Zapped me pretty hard with electricity."

Eva tabbed her own jaw. "Looks like she got in a good blow, too."

That pain had been masked by the rest of the agony my body had undergone. I should have asked the healer to patch that up, too, so that I didn't have to go round looking like a punch bag. Oh, well, too late now. I rolled my head round to look at Eva.

"Yeah. I don't want to think about what she would have done if Rathbone hadn't shown up."

"He asked me where you were earlier," she said.

"He was Bevan's messenger. Wanted to tell me the bloody druid enforcer academy was offering me a spot to study with them for a few weeks."

"What? That's insane." Her tone of excitement plummeted when our gazes met. "And I'm guessing not a good thing."

"People like us don't get to join the enforcers. We aren't druids, and centuries of elitist bullshit isn't going to disappear. No matter how hopeful Bevan is that I'm somehow the golden child of change."

"I'm guessing you said no."

I rolled onto my side and winced. "You don't really think I'd say yes to that—to spending more time with the people who mistreated my brother? I've been trying to stay under the radar here, which seems to be impossible. Being the only one who wasn't a druid there would make things a thousand times worse."

"Not even if it meant getting close to people who could point you in the direction of a certain enforcer?" Her exaggerated wink had the intended effect and I snickered, and then got serious again.

"Not even then. Besides, I don't want to be an enforcer. I don't know what I really want but I know it's not that."

"Well, you told Bevan to shove it and you don't have to make any other decisions right now." She pushed herself off the edge of the bed and turned the lock on the door leading out into the common area. "And Celine isn't getting in here. So you should get some rest."

On cue, a yawn escaped my lips and I stretched my arms up over my head. Apparently getting the crap kicked out of you, and then getting healed up, was exhausting.

"Did you find whatever you were looking for, for your mum?" I murmured as I shed my uniform and crawled beneath the blankets.

"No." The finality with which she said that word made it clear we weren't going to discuss whatever was going on with her. I rolled over and stared at the wall, trying to calm my thoughts and body enough to sleep. I didn't need to be haunted by the encounter with Celine. Just thinking about it made phantom bursts of electricity dance down my arms, tickling the tiny hairs.

I didn't know if manifesting your desires was a real thing but as I closed my eyes, I tried to focus entirely on that fantasy future with Zachary. If I wanted it bad enough in my dreams, maybe, just maybe, he'd be there waiting for me when the world fell away.

Chapter Seven

Someone was definitely watching out for me. It had been nearly two months since Bevan had blindsided me with the offer from the enforcer academy and he hadn't pestered me about it again. Instructor Rathbone hadn't, either. In fact, he barely acknowledged that it happened. I did catch him watching me in Energy Manipulation, little worry lines creasing his forehead as his gaze darted between Celine and me. She, too, had been leaving me alone. Some of the whispering behind my back had even died down.

"Did you hear about this weekend?" Eva asked as we settled into Unique Magics the Wednesday before Halloween.

"What's going on this weekend?"

"Some of the third years are throwing a party on the grounds. Now that the third-floor corridor isn't cursed, they're going to use that space. It's going to be huge. It's Bevan approved and everything."

I glanced around the room at our classmates. I spent enough time with them as it was. I didn't have any desire to spend it with them recreationally, too. Besides, it wasn't like I had a great track record with parties. Especially ones around Halloween. I didn't think I'd be forgetting the last one any time soon, more was the pity. But I didn't want to be a total buzz kill, either. It was nice to see Eva excited about something other than studying.

"Well, I guess that's a good thing," I muttered, hoping Instructor Glover would appear and start the lesson before this conversation could go where I thought it was going. "Let people blow off some steam."

"We should go," Eva said, nudging my shoulder.

"I don't know," I said with a sigh. So much for Glover rescuing me. "I've not been in a party mood lately."

"You've been in a moping mood," she said, quirking an eyebrow. "And I know you haven't tried reaching out to Zachary like you promised. Girl, you need some happiness in your life. A party is just the thing."

"Is it, though? I mean by my estimation half the people here hate me and the other half either tolerate me or have some weird admiration for me. Either way, it's super awkward being around anyone but you. And it's not like I'm going to just go get hammered."

"I'm not saying you get blackout drunk. But a drink or two isn't going to hurt. Besides, it's going to be a good time. And anyway, it's tradition."

I didn't have time to either come up with a decent excuse (unfortunately), or dig myself in any deeper (fortunately), before Instructor Glover appeared from the corridor.

"All right, everyone, I know you're all abuzz about the Halloween festivities this weekend, but we've still got a few more days to go to get there. So let's focus on what we're here to learn. Control of your unique magics."

That sounded better to me right now than it ever had before. Anything to get Eva off the subject of the party, and her weird insistence that I attend. In that moment, an unpleasant thought occurred to me. I gnawed at my lip while I thought it over. She wasn't wrong that I hadn't been making much of an effort to reach out to Zachary. But had she been doing some snooping on her own? Had she secretly invited him to the party, in the hopes that he and I would see each other and rekindle... whatever it was we'd had? For someone who could sniff out a lie and a secret from miles off, my roommate was too good at hiding her own.

I did my best to put the stupid Halloween party out of my head and focus on Glover's words. Like we had every class before, we pushed the desk to the sides of the room and stood in the centre, letting our bodies relax. I used to be able to do it so easily, thanks in no small part to all the extra lessons she'd given me last year, but today my body was being stubborn. I knew it had to be all in my head, but my back muscles twitched in the same pattern they had the night Celine had hit me with her energy blast.

Except the healers had taken care of that. It was just psychosomatic. Which was ridiculous, because I'd been in this class plenty of times since she'd attacked me. The thought of the coming party—and the one we'd had last year—really had me rattled.

"Come on, Norah," I ground out under my breath. "Focus."

I was being ridiculous. I knew that. This whole hang up was ridiculous. And I needed to get over it.

But there was no way I was going to actually be able to do anything in class today if I didn't let the tension and stress out of my body. So I blew out a slow breath and shook my hands. I felt vertebrae pop in my neck as I turned it side to side and a small sigh escaped my lips. I could sense the magic within me, longing to be let loose. It rippled just below the surface. It had taken me more than a year to feel it that way and now I didn't trust myself to be able to do much of anything magical until that ripple passed through me from head to toe.

"All right everyone, you all know the drill by now," Glover called, pulling me from my meditation.

I took my time opening my eyes and pulling my desk back to its usual spot. Eva wandered off across the room to sit with the other students whose unique powers were more mental than physical and then I was alone. The rest of the class clustered as far from me as they could get.

Which was fine by me. If I didn't have to interact with them, all the better.

As I sat there trying to conjure even the tiniest of shadows and failing, I felt their silent judgment. To them, not only had I barged in on their special class late in the semester last year, but I wasn't even good enough to be here. I couldn't conjure things consistently. And I'd only ever really made big displays of power a couple times. There wasn't any rhyme or reason to it.

There's no way those druids would want me in their stupid academy if they knew how shit I am at magic.

As I sat there, trying to will the shadows out of my body, a very real shadow fell across my desk and I hesitated, then turned to find its owner. Instructor Glover stood beside me.

"What's the problem, Norah?" Her voice was low, pitched just for my ears.

I still caught my classmates snickering behind my back, no doubt loving the fact that I needed special attention from the instructor. Again.

"Everything's fine," I answered.

"Don't lie to me. The frustration is written all over your face."

I didn't want this kind of attention. Couldn't she just let me struggle? Give me a low grade if she had to? Why did she need to single me out in front of everyone?

"It's nothing, really. I just don't think my head's in it today, is all."

"I know I gave you extra lessons last year, but I can't do that again," she said before walking away and weaving her way through the other students.

I stared after her, my mind trying to process her words. She wasn't trying to give me special treatment after all. She was going to let me fail all on my own. Well, fine. That was what I wanted, wasn't it? A part of me tail spun straight into panic, screaming that I needed her to come back and fix me. To tell me why I couldn't control my powers like everyone else. Even the people whose powers weren't clearly defined were doing it better than me.

I sat there, stewing in my own inward hatred of my magic. I'd spent so long wanting to be rid of it, then when it appeared in full force I'd wanted to understand it and embrace it. But it didn't want to be understood. Not by me. It just... it wasn't fair! And sure, I was an adult, and I was too damned old to believe in fairy tales like 'fair', but why did it have to be so unfair anyway?

The rest of the lesson passed by in a blur and before I knew it, Instructor Glover dismissed us with an assignment I didn't quite catch. Probably because I hadn't listened to a single thing outside of my own self-pity since she'd walked away from my desk. Served me right. I'd have to ask Eva to explain it to me when we were back in the dorm. I snatched up my things and tossed them in my bag as she joined me.

"I really think a party would do you some good," she said, by way of greeting.

"Backstabbers aren't invited," Celine said loudly as she walked by without breaking her stride.

Don't rise to it, Norah, I warned myself. *It's what she wants. Ignore her. Count to ten. Just don't rise to it.*

I opened my mouth to tell her to go to hell when someone beat me to it. "And who says she's a backstabber?"

Reggie took a step forward, placing himself between me and Celine. I narrowed my eyes. What was with him always popping up lately? We'd never even spoken last year, at least, not that I could recall. I mean, it was kind of flattering that he was being so vocal about his support of me, I supposed—whatever his reasons might be—but why did he care so much about someone he'd never even properly met? Even in the last month or two we'd barely spoken a word.

"It's obvious, isn't it?" Celine said, her voice haughty. "She ruined everything. She's not welcome at the party."

"It isn't your party," he said, crossing his arms over his chest. "You don't get to decide who goes and who doesn't."

"Oh, don't I?" She cut a cold smirk over his shoulder at me. "I know the people throwing it. If I tell them to make the guest list more exclusive, they will."

"Well, you don't have to worry," I snapped. "I'm not going to your stupid party."

All eyes landed on me. It was like they'd forgotten was still there. They'd been arguing about me without recognising I still existed. Wasn't that just lovely?

"You can't let her bully you into staying away," Reggie argued. His eyes pleaded with me to reconsider my stance.

"I'm not," I said with a shrug. "I wasn't going anyway."

I eyed Celine. She and her friends were blocking the exit of the classroom into the corridor, and I caught Glover standing behind her desk looking annoyed at the bottleneck. Or maybe she was just irritated that petty schoolyard drama was unfolding in her classroom when she had better things to do. Which made two of us.

I started to shoulder past Celine when she stepped in front of me.

"You are so pathetic, Norah. You can't even fight your own battles. You have to be rescued. Let's hope he's around to keep an eye on you next time, too." She gave me a condescending smirk before pivoting on her heel and marching out of the room.

I bit down hard on my tongue to keep from telling her what I really thought. I didn't need to get in trouble for cussing her out in front of the entire class. Mostly because I knew if I got started, I wasn't going to be able to stop and it would only make the situation worse. She hadn't attacked me again since that day in the corridor, and I didn't need to provoke her. Not when I had so little control over my own magic to defend myself with.

I waited for the rest of the students to filter out before I left the room. I had a free period now and I was headed back to the dorm. I needed to figure out why my magic was so erratic, and I didn't want to do that with an audience.

Unfortunately, someone fell into step beside me and when they didn't start trash talking Celine, I knew it wasn't Eva. I looked over to find Reggie matching my stride.

"Look, I appreciate you sticking up for me," I started before he interrupted.

"She had no right to say those awful things to you."

"It's not new. She's always been a bitch to me. I can handle it."

"But you shouldn't have to."

"Maybe not, but that's just what my life is. And as much as it's nice to have someone who has my back, you aren't doing me any favours. It's not that I don't appreciate you caring, because believe me, I really do." I shook my head. "But she'll just use the fact that I've had to have a guy step in to defend me against me. She'll think I'm weak and that's ten times worse than letting her call me names or kick me out of parties I wasn't going to anyway."

He hung his head as we walked along the corridor. Great. Way to go, Norah. Now I'd managed to offend one of the few people who actually had my back around here. I swallowed a groan, and headed for the stairs. Reggie trailed behind me.

"I didn't mean it like that, I swear," he murmured, and when I turned to look at him, his cheeks burned red.

"I know. You were trying to help. And I think I'm not used to people wanting to do that. It's still new and, well, I don't do all that great with new."

"You know she can't actually bar you from the party," he said with a smirk.

"She'll definitely try. She's got influence with the older students and there are a lot of people who believe in what she was trying to accomplish."

He shook his head, looking earnest.

"Not even she's that powerful. You could get in if you went with someone… someone like me."

I stopped walking and he made it a few more paces before he realised I wasn't beside him and stopped. I studied him in those few moments. He seemed like a nice enough guy, but I really wasn't interested in going to the party. Besides, if Eva was keeping a Zachary-sized secret from me, it wouldn't do to show up on some other guy's arm. That sent the wrong message. Even if I was still confused about what I wanted the right message to be if I did see him again. Then again, fostering a little jealousy in the druid's heart might not be the worst thing in the world, because I clearly wasn't on his mind right now. I dismissed the thought as quickly as it came. I didn't need him mad at me, too.

"It wouldn't be a date," he said, his face falling mid-sentence. That was obviously exactly what he'd been hoping it would be. He pressed on, speaking too quickly so his words tumbled together. "Just a couple of friends going together, you know, just as friends."

I had to let him down easy. As annoying and potentially dangerous him defending me was, he'd done it with the best of intentions, and he deserved better than being hurt just because I was having a bad day. I forced an apologetic smile.

"Oh, that's really nice of you. But I really wasn't planning on going. I need to study. I'm still so far behind everyone else in lessons, especially unique magics. I mean, you saw me today. I couldn't even conjure anything. I really should be focusing on improving my skills."

I was rambling, and we both knew it. I tried to not look like a total idiot as I reached out and patted his arm. "But I do really appreciate the offer. And you having my back."

"I'm here for whatever you need," he said, eagerness pitching his voice up a few notes.

"Thanks." I pulled my hand away from his arm.

"I'll always have your back, Norah," he said as I rushed off down the stairs to the dorm.

How had I gotten here? I was pining for a guy I could probably never have and another perfectly decent guy was clearly flirting with me. I didn't need to be the centre of some weird love triangle. Not when I had to be on my guard against Celine and her posse. Even if I didn't show up at that stupid party, they were going to keep coming for me. If I could just crack this problem, just make my magic more reliable, then I'd be able to hold my own the next time they came for me. Because there would be a next time, that I was sure of. My shadows had protected me from the worst of her assault last time, but there was no way I could replicate it. Not yet, anyway. I hadn't been intending to actually study during the party, but I should probably take the opportunity while the whole academy was preoccupied with something other than making my life hell to actually figure it out.

Because if I didn't, I had a feeling I'd have far more to

worry about than flunking Unique Magics.

Chapter Eight

Halloween snuck up on me. I'd been doing everything I could to ignore the whole affair and my efforts might have paid off just a little too well. Six hours before the party was supposed to kick off, Eva and I were sitting in the library, sequestered at one of the corner tables that overlooked the grounds. Through the window, I could spot little lanterns lining the walkways. Probably Bevan's effort to be festive.

I drummed my left index finger on the cover of my botany textbook and bit back a growl of frustration. I didn't understand how learning about bloody plants could be so hard. Somehow, I was still behind the rest of the class, even though I'd been learning the same material at the same pace as everyone else since last year, which was just irritating. It wasn't like this even involved casting any actual magic. Apparently my powers of suckiness extended beyond just practical classes. It figured that the one thing I'd excel at was failing.

"You look miserable," Eva said from across the table.

"You would be, too, if you were destined to fail at keeping stupid plants alive."

"You know that's not what I meant," she said, arching a brow.

"If you think I'm feeling down about not going to this party, you're wrong. I don't care who's going to be there."

"I just hate to think of you sitting around by yourself while literally the whole academy is off partying." She sighed, propping her chin in her right hand, and a couple of twists of dark hair fell off her shoulder to frame her face.

I snorted. "Please. After a drink or two, you won't be thinking about me at all."

"I could never forget you, you're too much of a headache," she teased, and then the concerned look shadowed her face again. "Are you sure you won't reconsider? You've been working so hard lately. You deserve a little fun."

That might be true, but there was no way I would consider this party 'fun'. Not when the whole academy would be there to judge me. I was pretty sure most of the people here still hated me and I didn't need to be reminded of it. Not in a place where tempers flaring could cause real damage.

"I'm good," I said, forcing what I hoped was a convincing smile. "Honestly. You go and have fun. You're planning to wear the purple dress, right?"

Her lips pressed together in a worried line. "It's too much, isn't it?"

"No. It's perfect. You're going to look amazing in it."

I wasn't generally envious of other people, but I did wish I had my roommate's sense of style. And control of her magic. And general lack of concern for other people's opinions of her. Yeah, okay, there was a reason I hung out with Eva so much. She was pretty awesome.

"Just promise me you're not going to sit here all night," she said.

I held up my right hand. "I swear I will not spend all night in the library. Besides," I added, dropping my hand, "I figure if I haven't absorbed the knowledge at this point, it isn't likely to happen."

Eva just shook her head and snickered at my educational misfortune before packing her books up. "Okay, well, I'll see you in the morning… unless we get a repeat of last year."

I wagged a finger at her. "Don't you dare jinx this."

She held up her hands in a pleading gesture and backed away from me. The smile slowly slipped from my face as she left. Halloween last year still ranked amongst my worst days ever, and it would be a long time before the memories of what happened faded, taking the pain with them. It would be a long time before the look on my brother's face as he was sentenced to incarceration at Daoradh stopped being the last thing I saw before I went to sleep each night. That hadn't been what Eva had been talking about, though. She'd meant when Celine and her sycophantic followers attacked me—also not a highlight of my life—and Zachary had come charging in to save the day. My hands still tingled from the memory of his touch. It was cringe-worthy and sappy and romantic, but it was true just the same.

I sat there in the silence of the library, replaying memories—good and bad—for a solid fifteen minutes before I shook off the lethargy and tossed my books into my bag. I wasn't the worrying-about-girls-who-attacked-me and pining-over-guys-who-rescued-me sort. For one thing, as I'd told my newfound admirer, I didn't need to be rescued.

The excitement on the rest of the grounds was palpable as I made my way down to the canteen to grab a coffee and a snack to keep myself going. I really should study. I meant what I'd said to Eva about the Botany stuff—if that hadn't sunk in by now, it wasn't likely to. But I could practise energy manipulation or harnessing my shadows in the privacy of my dorm room and with everyone else occupied, even if I lost control, there'd be no one there to see or judge. That seemed like a pretty compelling argument to me. Plus I wouldn't risk bumping into any well-meaning instructors wondering why I wasn't at the party. Win-win.

When I stepped into the dorm, I could see that Eva had changed her mind about the purple dress. In fact, she'd scribbled a little note and pinned it to the sleeve. I bent to read her handwriting; *Just seems too much.*

I set my coffee down on my desk and slung my bag onto the end of my bed, then nibbled the half of the pasty I'd managed to restrain myself from eating on the walk back here. Crumbs flaked into my lap, but I didn't care. It was dumb, but it felt freeing to just sit there without worrying about what other people thought of me. And while I sat there finishing off the snack, I remembered that there was another person I knew wouldn't judge me.

I'd truly meant to reach out to Kelsey sooner, but I'd given myself all kinds of excuses for why I'd kept putting it off. She was busy. *I* was busy. She didn't need a Misfits student pestering her with academy drama. But she had made the offer to be there if I needed a friend and as much as I didn't want to admit it to Eva, a tiny part of me was sad not to be going to the party tonight, to just act like a normal student for once and hang out with the rest of my year.

I dug into the bottom of my bag until I found the communication stone she'd given me last year. I cupped it in my palms for a moment without doing anything else. Even though no one had specifically told me it was prohibited or restricted, I always felt like I was breaking some rule by using it. Especially to contact a druid. And really especially one who was a member of the Druid

Council.

"Get over yourself, Norah," I muttered and settled back against the pillow, downing the remnants of the coffee before closing my eyes.

It had been months since I'd done this, but I still remembered. I concentrated, picturing Kelsey's face in my mind's eye. I held the stone up to my mouth and said, "Kelsey". Silence greeted me and my ears strained to catch any hint of sound.

I counted my own heartbeats.

One.

Two.

Three.

Four…

"Norah?" Kelsey's voice broke through and my eyes shot open.

"Uh, hi," I blurted. *Idiot.*

"It's been a while. Is everything okay?" The communication stone didn't give much away in terms of ambient noise, but she sounded distracted.

"It's… complicated."

"What's going on?"

"Short version; half the academy hates me for what I did. The girls I stopped from overthrowing the academy blame me for their poor life choices and literally every student here except me is currently getting sloshed at an academy-wide party." *And I'm having guy drama.*

"Oh dear," she said after a pause. "That does seem like quite a lot for one person to deal with."

"I know you're probably busy and have a lot more important things to deal with than my drama, but honestly I could use a friendly ear."

"You can always reach out," she said, and I could hear the smile in her voice. She didn't sound nearly as timid as she had when we'd first got to know each other last year. Maybe she was settling into her role at Circle headquarters.

"I don't know, Kelsey." I tried to keep the sigh out of my voice. "I guess part of me has been questioning why I'm even here. I still can't get my magic to work right. Not like everyone else."

Kelsey was quiet for a beat and then said, "Well, that is kind of the point of going to Braeseth, isn't it? To learn to control it?"

Curse her and her logic.

"I just wish I knew why my magic worked sometimes, and then other times... nothing. I'm always chasing the others, trying to catch up, and honestly? I'm terrified that I never will." A shudder ran through me, raising the little hairs on my arms. "I'm a failure, Kelsey. And a fraud."

"From what I've heard, you are far from either of those things," she replied. "You are still learning to harness and control your gifts. It is worth the struggle, Norah. You may not believe it, but you've shown amazing bravery in the face of overwhelming odds. I've read all the reports about what happened last year. You inspire me."

I sat there in the empty dorm room, communication stone lying heavy in my hands, and stared at it in shock. She'd pushed me not to give up on believing I could do things before, but this felt different.

"I… I don't know what to say," I mumbled, glad she couldn't see my face glowing pink.

"You don't have to say anything. I just wanted you to know that you have people in your corner. And I believe you will figure out your magic. You manifested these powers for a reason. It's not clear to you why, yet, but you'll get there."

There it was: her hint of infectious optimism underneath the insecurity she projected to the rest of the world. I clutched that tiny nugget of belief in my chest and tried to let it take root within me. She was right. I could figure this out. But I didn't need to do it right this second. I closed my eyes, and a smile trickled over my lips.

Everyone deserved to have a little fun and let loose. And if there was an academy-sanctioned venue to do so, I should take advantage of it. I eyed the dress Eva had left behind and couldn't help but wonder if she'd known I would eventually change my mind. That woman was practically psychic.

"Norah, are you still there?" Kelsey's voice drifted in and out.

I cleared my throat. "Yeah. Just thinking I might actually try to be social for a change."

"That sounds like a good idea."

As I slid off the bed and reached for the dress, I pictured Zachary in his dress shirt back on Valentine's Day. He had looked so handsome. "This may be a stupid question, but do you know what happened to the enforcers who were here at Braeseth last year?"

"You mean the ones who went rogue?"

"No, the others. The ones who tried to stop them."

Kelsey's chuckle seemed to make the stone vibrate in my palm. "Do I get the feeling you might be asking about one enforcer in particular?"

My cheeks flushed red again and I was grateful all over again that she couldn't see my embarrassment. It was better that way. I reached for the dress, fumbling with the pin to remove the note. "Hey, if I put the stone down, am I going to lose you?"

"As long as it's within a short distance of you, I should still be able to hear you," she said.

Good. That somewhat lessened the chance of me

accidentally stabbing myself. I set the stone down on Eva's bed and slipped the pin out, injury-free. I shimmied out of my own clothes and pulled the dress on over my head. It was a pretty good fit, considering we weren't the exact same body type—she really had a knack for choosing clothes that were more than a little flattering. This was much classier than my usual look.

"So, was I wrong in thinking you're inquiring about a particular enforcer?" Kelsey's tone turned coy, almost like she was falling into gossip mode.

"Maybe," I admitted as I smoothed the fabric over my abdomen, and then glanced down at my feet. I knew that no matter what sort of magic might exist, Eva and I were not the same shoe size.

I rummaged in my own clothes for a pair of acceptable shoes and finally happened on a plain black pair without heels—because tonight's aim was to *not* utterly humiliate myself in front of the entire academy for a change, and it wasn't like I got a whole lot of practice walking in heels. Or anything that wasn't a pair of trainers, come to that. No wonder Eva despaired of my wardrobe.

"Well, I can't say that I've seen him around headquarters at all, but I know that he got some recognition for his part in stopping the attack."

It wasn't the news I'd been hoping for on the Zachary

front, the first bit, at least, but it was all I was likely to get. I still couldn't shake the thought that Eva had tracked him down and invited him tonight, and that was why she'd been so insistent I went. There was only one way to find out if I was right.

"Well, not that I'm being like a stalker or anything, but if you happen to run into him, could you let him know that I…" What did I want her to tell him? Sure, I missed him and I wanted to see him and talk to him, but I didn't want to come across as clingy.

"If I see him, I'll let him know you've asked after him. How's that?"

"Perfect."

"I should let you get ready for your night," Kelsey said softly. There was a longer pause this time and then, "I really am glad you reached out. I thought about doing it first, but I didn't want to intrude. I didn't want you thinking I was prying."

I couldn't help but smile at her words. We were more alike than I thought. "I promise it won't be another six months before I call again," I said.

"I'll hold you to that." I could hear the hint of a smile in her tone, and then she was gone.

The stone went dark on the bed beside me as I straightened the straps on the dress. I stowed the stone back in my bag and checked the time. The party was still in the early hours. There was a good chance I could actually enjoy myself before the night was over.

I stopped at the door and caught a glimpse of my reflection in the mirror by her bed. No make-up, and my hair was a mess. Eva would murder me if I went out in her dress not looking like I belonged in it. I doubled back to the bathroom and found Eva's make-up kit still sitting by the sink. I tugged my hair down from its messy bun and dragged a comb through it. I was no miracle worker with hair—I'd had more pressing concerns for the better part of my teenaged life—so I settled on pulling it half up and into a twist with a clip. It would do.

With that settled, I threw on some eyeliner and blush and a touch of shadow in the corners—I was rubbish at the whole smoky eye look—and called it good. I was about to step out of the bathroom when I plucked the slender tube of lip liner off the sink and dabbed a light coat on. I might not be planning to kiss anyone tonight, but it didn't hurt to be prepared, right?

"Go knock them dead," I told my reflection with a smile before heading for the corridor that until last semester had been off limits. It couldn't be any worse than last year, right?

Chapter Nine

I really had *got* to stop thinking those words.

I stopped at the third-floor landing for a moment and let myself imagine that Zachary truly was waiting for me at the party, hoping that I'd walk through the door. We'd laugh about the fact we hadn't seen or spoken in months, and we'd enjoy the music and the drinks. There might even be a goodnight kiss in it for him.

Reality is a real bitch sometimes.

I pushed through the door and into the corridor, and immediately the electrical current in the air made my hair stand on end. Thin dark tendrils practically vibrated with energy as I stood there. I licked the tips of my fingers to smooth the frizz down, but it only made it worse. *Great.* Maybe people wouldn't notice that my hair looked a mess by the time I got to the party.

I perked up at the sound of music coming from down the corridor and I picked up my pace. The press of electricity in the air tried to drag me to a halt, and the hairs on the back of my neck stood on end—either because of the electricity, or the realisation welling in the pit of my stomach. This wasn't just some strange interference, or a side effect of so many people gathered in one place. Someone was doing this.

"I thought we made it clear you weren't welcome," Celine's voice sounded from behind me.

The smart thing to do would be to ignore her. She didn't have the authority to tell me where I could or couldn't go, not if I didn't let her. Despite what she seemed to think, she did not run this academy, and she didn't get to control me.

But if I walked away, I'd never hear the end of it. I'd already heard the not-so-quiet whispers about needing a guy to stand up for me. If she thought I was running from her, she'd make sure the whole academy was calling me a coward by the end of the night. And for all of my big talk, I *did* care what they thought of me. And as much as I might like to delude myself into believing her name-calling wouldn't bother me, hearing those words at every corner would eat away at me. I had no choice but to face her.

That, and I didn't like giving her a clear shot at my back.

I turned slowly to find Celine in a low cut dress that exposed more cleavage than I'd ever wanted to see. The hemline barely came to her mid-thigh. I wasn't one for slut shaming—that was a low blow in my books—but how she moved around without completely falling out of the fabric was a mystery that defied every drop of magic inside these walls. Miranda and Jessa flanked her in equally skimpy outfits. The irritating thing was how well they carried them off.

"You made it perfectly clear," I answered her as calmly as I could. "But since you don't run this academy, I'm choosing to ignore you."

Celine advanced a step or two, the staccato clicks of her heels echoing around the corridor. "I didn't really think you'd be stupid enough to show your face."

"Stupid?" I shook my head. "That's not what I'd call standing up to bullies. That's all you are, Celine. You may think you're in charge here, but you're not. You're no better than anyone else."

"Bold words from a traitor," Jessa snapped.

I could still see the faintest of scars on her lips from where Celine had used magic to shut her up last year, and she'd obviously never dared get the wound treated. Why she put up with Celine's abuse was beyond me. I couldn't be the only one to see what she was. On Celine's other side, Miranda glared at me, arms crossed over her chest.

"In case you forgot," I ground out, "I saved your lives."

"That's right," Celine said, a sneer contorting her heavily made-up face. "You're the golden girl. The *hero.*"

"I'm not. I didn't ask for any of that," I said, taking a small step back. The memories of what had happened last time we were alone in a corridor together were all too fresh, and this time, I didn't think anyone would be coming along to save me.

"You just keep telling yourself that, Norah," Celine hissed as she closed the distance between us. Her normally vibrant red locks looked the colour of dried blood as she moved so close to me that I could feel her breath on my cheek. "I'm going to fix that."

"Get out of my face," I said.

"Not until we've given you a little lesson in respect," she snarled, and slammed a fist into my stomach.

Except when I staggered backwards, clutching at my belly, I noticed her hands weren't anywhere near me. An electrical current coursed across her body, forming into a solid mass in front of her. I'd never seen anyone manifest their magic like that before.

"You'll like this," she purred. "I picked it up while we suffered in prison, where you sent us." Her manifested electricity shot forward, wrapped around my throat, and squeezed.

Dark spots danced in my vision, and I could feel the energy burning my skin. I thought I caught the scent of smouldering meat and even if I'd wanted to gag, my throat wasn't responding to my brain's commands. Panic took hold of me, and darkness shot out of my hands, knocking Celine off balance. Her energy tried to clamp down harder on my throat, but the sudden attack was enough to throw her magic off kilter. It faded and I gasped for air, flailing for anything solid to support me. My fingers brushed the wall and I pressed my back to it.

"Nice try, traitor," Jessa said, her mouth twisting into a nasty smile. "But you're outnumbered."

"And outpowered," Celine added, a malevolent glint in her eye as she straightened.

My throat burned both inside and out but I managed to suck in some small gasps of air, enough to clear my vision, and my panic. I needed to protect myself.

Celine and her cronies came at me as one, magic flaring from three sets of fingertips at once. I threw my arms up to cover my face and neck, leaving my core woefully exposed. I didn't have any other options. If I took too many hits to the head, there was zero chance I'd be able to protect myself. At least if I only got hit in the torso, I'd still have a shot at remaining conscious. And if I was conscious, I could fight back.

I tensed, waiting for the attack, but Celine and her friends vanished from view. I blinked, but the wall of black remained in front of me. Panic flared in my gut. Had they blinded me? I held out a hand and pressed it gently against the barrier in front of me. It was solid matter, but it felt reassuringly familiar. Relief quelled the panic. My shadows had come out to protect me.

"Your pathetic shadows won't save you for long,"

Celine's voice called from somewhere on my left.

As much as I hated to admit it, she was right about that. My shadow magic was so erratic, I still had no idea how to control it, or why it seemed to respond on an almost subconscious level at some times, and there was barely a flicker at others. They were right about something else, too. I was outpowered and outnumbered.

I felt the edges of the shadow wall begin to falter and then it began to disintegrate, burned away by their magic. I didn't know what sort of spell they were weaving, but it was strong, and my shadows were no match for it. I tried to feed more power into my defence, but I didn't really know how. The efforts made me woozy and the world started to spin. I took as deep a breath as my injured throat would allow, readying myself for more attacks the moment my magic failed.

The darkness faded all at once, leaving me temporarily dazzled by the light of the corridor. I was utterly defenceless against them and they took full advantage. Zaps of electricity lanced over my body, setting nerve endings on fire, sending me to my knees. I grit my teeth as best I could to avoid biting off my own tongue and because I'd be damned if I was going to give any of them the satisfaction of hearing me scream.

Something thumped into my back, pushing me to the floor, and I didn't fight. It was taking everything I had just to keep from crying out in pain, and I had nothing left. My magic was gone. All I had was my will to get through whatever they were going to do. They wouldn't kill me. I would survive. And then I'd find a way to pay them back.

A thunderous crash echoed through the corridor around me and I heard something—several somethings—collide with the walls beyond me. I squinted down the hallway through eyes that were almost swollen shut and just barely made out the advancing figure of Instructor Glover as she strode down it and stopped in front of me.

"If you three so much as touch another student on these grounds," she spat, her voice cracking around me like a whip, "I will see to it that you are expelled."

Sonic waves rippled out from her fingertips, caressing my battered body as if she were projecting some sort of shield. I couldn't see much, but I heard another set of footsteps approaching.

"Norah? What happened?" Rathbone's voice was soft, brimming with concern. His hands eased me off the floor and into a sitting position.

The click-clack of Celine's shoes disappeared down the far end of the corridor and I slumped against Rathbone's shoulder. Relief flooded me, leaving me even more drained.

"What happened?" Rathbone repeated softly.

My breathing rattled in my damaged throat but when Instructor Glover answered, I realised he hadn't expected me to answer. "They jumped her. Honestly, I told Bevan it was reckless to let them come back."

"We've had this debate and now isn't the time to rehash it," Rathbone said, his voice tight with frustration. "Norah, can you stand?"

I tried to say 'I'm not sure', but it came out a garbled mess. Still, I managed to rise to my feet without faceplanting. That was better than I'd expected.

"I'll get her to the infirmary," Rathbone said.

"I'm going to speak to the dean," Glover said. "This cannot continue."

I opened my mouth to object, but nothing other than a wheezing came out, and I doubted anything I had to say was going to stop her, anyway. I snapped my mouth shut again as her footsteps hurried away.

"Are you ready?" Rathbone asked after a long moment. I nodded, and his hand squeezed my shoulder lightly. "Let's go, then. Take your time."

I didn't have much choice in that, and we made our way to the medwing at a painstakingly slow pace. This route was becoming far more familiar than I would have liked. So much for keeping my head down and staying out of trouble this year.

Rathbone pushed the door open with the hand that

wasn't currently resting on my back, presumably waiting for me to faint, and I shuffled inside. A healer looked up from behind her desk, did a double take—which wasn't especially flattering—and hurried over to us.

"You're going to be okay," Rathbone said softly, and I was glad at least one of us believed that.

"Miss Sheehan, back again?" The female healer from last month sounded genuinely sorry to see me standing there.

I forced myself to swallow the pain enough to speak. "Wish I wasn't."

"No doubt. On the bed, please."

She gestured to a bed against one wall and I shuffled over to it, Rathbone hovering protectively in my shadow. I perched on the edge, not daring to lie down. If I passed out, there was no way they'd let me out of here tonight, and I didn't want to spend more time here than I had to. It was far too quiet, for one thing. Too much time to think.

"I'm just going to touch your throat," the healer said, and before I could object, she probed my sore throat. "It doesn't feel like anything's broken, so that's a good sign."

"Hurts to breathe," I managed.

Through the puffy slits that were my eyes, I could see her nod her head. "Does anything else feel like it's broken?"

I took a moment to assess the aches in my body. I could still move everything without it screaming in agony, which I figured was a good sign. "No."

"Good. I'm going to give you something to ease the pain, and then we'll see about treating these other injuries."

She strode through a set of curtains at the back of the room and disappeared from sight. I heard a scraping beside me and twisted round to see Rathbone settling into a chair beside my bed. Great. Just what I needed. Sure, he meant well, but I didn't need to be babysat. I scowled at him, or at least, I tried to, but I didn't have full control of most of my face.

"Don't you have someplace better to be?" I demanded.

"Nope."

I sighed and slumped back against the wall behind me. We sat like that for a while before he spoke again.

"You shouldn't be afraid to ask for help, Norah. I meant it before. If you need help or support, you can always come to me."

For all the good that would have done. It wasn't like he could watch me twenty-four hours a day, and nor did I want him to. If Celine wanted to get to me—and she clearly did—then she would, and nothing anyone could do was going to change that. And certainly not me getting a reputation for hiding behind lecturers.

Rathbone nodded, his hands resting heavily on his legs, and he exhaled deeply.

"Yeah, I thought that might be your response. But the offer stands, okay? Even if you just want to talk. Anything you say to me goes no further, not if you don't want it to. You don't have to deal with this alone."

The healer returned, much to my relief, and pressed a glass into my hands. "Drink this. All of it. I'm afraid it will taste terrible, but the effect will be almost instant."

I didn't argue. I guided the rim of the glass to my lips and downed it. Whatever was inside had a slight syrupy consistency but tasted like someone had thrown every citrus fruit under the sun into a blender and mixed it at top speed—then thrown in some mud for good measure. But the taste was soon the last thing on my mind. I'd barely set the glass down when my throat stopped seizing up, and swallowing was a pleasant numb sensation instead of feeling like the wolverine was shoving his hands down my throat.

"Lay back," the healer said, tapping my arm and taking my hand to touch the bed beneath me. "I'm going to get some healing balms to take care of the swelling and the other wounds."

Once she was gone again, I turned my head in the direction Rathbone had been sitting. "Look, it's not that

I'm not grateful, but I don't need an instructor swooping into save me every time I get into a scrape."

"Forgive me, Norah," Rathbone said, "but I wouldn't say this is a 'scrape'."

"I appreciate the support, really, but I can handle it myself. They got it out of their systems." I wasn't sure who I was trying to convince more—him, or me.

The healer cleared her throat and we both turned to look at her, although in my case it was fairly pointless because I could barely make out anything beyond a blurred outline.

"I'm going to need you to vacate the area," she said, presumably to the instructor because I was one hundred percent sure my presence here was mandatory.

"I'll wait outside," Rathbone said, but I shook my head.

"I'm fine. Please. I—" I screwed my eyes closed and took a moment to control my breathing. "If I change my mind, I'll come to you."

It wasn't that I didn't want to talk to someone. It was that I was worried if I started, I wouldn't be able to stop, and next thing I knew, I'd be spilling my guts about that time Micah turned my hippogryff doll into a warthog when we were kids. And I don't mean a warthog doll.

"Remember that my door is always open," Rathbone said, and then his footsteps receded.

"I'm going to need you to change out of your clothes," the healer said. "The balm is pretty sticky, and I'd hate to ruin your lovely dress."

I heard the metallic clang of a bowl being placed on the table beside the bed. I must be in worse shape than I thought if she needed an entire bowl of the stuff to address my injuries. And honestly, I'd thought I was in pretty bad shape to start with.

I let her help me out of the dress—which thankfully had survived the attack in better shape than I had, because if it had got ruined, I'd have been really pissed. Not to mention in Eva's bad books. She was going to be pissed enough that I ended up in the infirmary. So much for breaking the streak of bad things happening on Halloween. I sat in my underwear, shivering as the healer applied the balm to most of my body, chanting softly under her breath as she did. A moment after the chanting stopped, I felt her wrapping a hospital gown around me, and then she eased me back against the pillow and pressed a cool cloth that smelled of chamomile over my eyes.

"Get some rest. You'll feel better by the morning."

Her footsteps were soft on the floor as she retreated from my bed. The rest of the room was eerily silent around me. There never did seem to be many people here when I ended up occupying a bed. I laid there, letting the balm and spellcraft do their work. And as I finally slipped into unconsciousness, I couldn't shake the haunting resignation that once again, my magic had come out just enough to ensure I didn't die, but not enough to actually be useful.

I was never going to get the hang of this.

Chapter Ten

I awoke the following morning with a whole new appreciation for healers. Whatever magic she'd worked with the balm and chant, I was feeling stronger than I ever had. There wasn't a single ache or pain anywhere in my entire body. I could almost be grateful for the beating Celine and her groupies had given me if this was the result. Almost.

Like the night before, the infirmary was empty except for my bed, but it didn't feel quite as eerie in the morning light. I sat up and started to kick the blankets off when footsteps hurried toward me. I didn't recognise the face, but the uniform told me he was one of the academy healers.

"You need to rest," he insisted, clamping one hand on my shoulder to halt my escape attempt.

"I feel fine," I protested.

"Less than twenty-four hours is not enough time for the healing magic to finish its work," he said. "It's magic, not a miracle."

I heaved a dramatic sigh and flopped down against the pillow. He nodded his approval and moved away. As I lay there, contemplating how long I should wait before making a break for it, I caught the muffled sound of voices. They rose in pitch and intensity and it seemed like whoever was speaking was arguing, but I couldn't pick out individual words or voices. Then, a set of footsteps stalked my way and I tensed, only to relax when Eva appeared at my beside.

"I am so sorry," she said, throwing herself at me.

I braced myself as best I could to receive the weight of her body pulling me into an awkward embrace. Neither of us spoke for a minute as she just stood there, arms folded around my torso, her head resting on my shoulder.

"I'm okay," I managed as she finally released her grip and perched on the edge of the bed.

"You scared me half to death," she said, swatting my arm.

"Next time I get magically jumped, I'll be sure to let you know ahead of time," I said with an exaggerated roll of my eyes. It was good to see her.

Her face turned serious. "I mean it. I heard about it from Rathbone. He came to find me at the party last night and told me you'd been hurt. He didn't give me details but I knew who had done it."

"There's nothing you could have done," I replied.

"You don't know that. Maybe they wouldn't have tried anything if you had someone with you. They're not stupid. They wouldn't do anything like that with witnesses around."

"Maybe, but I can't go back and change it now. I'm just sorry you didn't get to see me in the dress you left me."

Eva looked at my bare arms and then cast around for any sign of the dress. "It didn't get ruined, did it?" Her cheeks darkened immediately as the words left her mouth. "Not that a dress is important compared to you nearly getting killed! I mean, that's not what I meant, I—"

"Eva, relax. It's fine. I'm fine. And so's the dress, by the way." I nodded to it and gave her a smile, but she twisted her hands together anxiously. We both knew it wasn't the dress she was worried about. "Look, I swear, I'm okay. It wasn't even that bad, I don't know why everyone's making such a fuss about it."

Her lips pressed together in a thin line like she wanted to call me on the lie, but instead she said,

"I would have come earlier, if they'd let me. They kept turning me away."

"It wouldn't have made a difference. That spell knocked me right out. I only just woke up."

I frowned, realising in that moment I had absolutely no idea what time it was. Bright light was streaming in through the window, but then, it was a big window.

"It's nearly lunchtime," Eva noted, as if she'd sensed my temporal confusion.

My stomach gurgled in response. I needed to get out

of here and get food. And clothes. Not necessarily in that order.

"If you want to assuage some of that illogical guilt of yours, you could convince the staff to let me out of here. And maybe get me some clothes?"

Because walking out of here with my head held high was going to be tricky if I was stuck in a hospital gown.

She bounced off the edge of the bed and marched off on a mission. I rested my head back against the pillow and closed my eyes. My mind was full of visions of the shadow wall I'd conjured yesterday, just as mysterious as when I'd manifested it in reality. If only I knew how it had happened and why it only worked sometimes.

"I promise, I will keep an eye on her and if it looks like she's got any problems, even a little one, I will bring her back myself," Eva said, her voice carrying across the empty room.

The healer didn't respond as she followed Eva back to my bed. He looked down at me, his forehead tight with disapproval.

"Are you absolutely certain you feel well enough to leave?"

I kicked off the blankets and got to my feet, trying to ignore the cool air against my exposed skin. "I feel great. Better than I did before it happened."

The healer narrowed his gaze at me. "I'm going to let

you go because I'm pretty sure if I don't, you're only going to sneak off the moment my back is turned."

I ducked my head and tried to quell the guilty flush spreading across my cheeks.

"And really, Miss Sheehan, try to stay out of here for a while."

"Believe me, I'd love nothing more," I said. "Starting right now."

"I'll be right back with some clean clothes," Eva said.

"Great."

She darted out the door and I sat back down on the edge of the bed to wait. The healer hovered nearby, occasionally chanting a spell in my direction and then jotting some notes on his clipboard.

"That should hold the healing magic in place until it's finished its work," he said, setting the clipboard aside just as Eva returned holding a pair of jeans and a top. The healer pulled the privacy curtain around me, and I heard him muttering something under his breath before his footsteps retreated. I traded my gown for the clothes and instantly felt warmer. I wondered if the healer had done something to warm me up as a parting gift. If so, I really needed to learn that spell. Braeseth could be draughty at the best of times.

"Come on, let's get some food in you. That will make you feel even better." Eva looped one arm through mine and led me into the corridor.

"You really shouldn't feel guilty," I told her as we walked. "It wasn't anyone's fault but theirs."

"I'm your friend. I should have realised you needed me. It was selfish to go to the party without you."

"Stop it," I snapped at her, dragged her to a halt and turning her to face me. "Don't you dare put yourself down on my account. You wanted to have a fun night. You're entitled have one."

She tugged on one of the twists that came down behind her left ear. "I just feel like you have such a target on your back, I need to be around in case you need me."

"You are the best friend I've ever had, Eva, you know that. But the fact that there are people who hate me shouldn't be the end of your social life."

She sighed. "I know, I just worry that something's going to happen and I'm going to lose my only friend."

I pulled her into a quick one-armed hug. "I promise I'm not looking for trouble. And I'm going to work harder to stay out of it."

"I'll hold you to that," she threatened, with a hint of a smile playing on her lips.

"Good, now come on. I'm starving."

The rest of the walk to the canteen was quick. I should have known the place would be busy serving students who hadn't long tumbled from their alcohol-induced lie-ins, but I hadn't really been thinking that far ahead. It looked like a funeral as we stepped into the room. Small clusters of students sat at tables, some with their heads resting on their arms as their friends tried to get them to eat something.

"Guess I missed a real rager," I said as we approached the line for food.

"I wouldn't be surprised if more people are still in bed sleeping it off," Eva said as she handed me a tray and a plate. "Do you just want to get something and eat it in the dorm?"

It wasn't a half-bad idea. I didn't need to be surrounded by so many hungover people. They said stupid things and my tolerance for dealing with their bullshit was at an all-time low today. But then I spotted Celine and her cronies standing in the food line.

My gaze met Celine's and held it, staring as intensely as I could until she blinked first. It was a small victory, but I'd take it.

"No, let's stay," I said. "I could use the air."

Eva snorted next to me. "You just don't want the bitch squad to see you get food and run."

"I liked my answer better," I replied before stepping down the line.

Celine reached the kitchen mage first and I noticed that neither her nor her entourage ordered much in the way of food. Good. I hoped I was ruining her appetite. I hoped that she was wondering right then what it would take to put me down, and keep me down. Because I didn't need her to see how close she'd come to breaking me last night.

I got to the front of the queue as the three of them stalked off to a table, watching me with what looked like a touch of wariness. I asked for a full English with extra everything from the mage, and he waved his hands, muttered a few words, and abruptly my plate was piled high with enough food to sustain a small army. Eva snorted her amusement and ordered a more sensible sized breakfast.

"I think you're going to explode if you eat all of that," Eva whispered in my ear. I shrugged a shoulder and grinned, leading us to a table where Celine couldn't miss me. I wanted her to know that she wasn't going to get rid of me that easily. There was only one thing bullies responded to, and it wasn't cowering away in my room. I was done with that. Even if it did mean letting the whole academy see me wrestling with my magic. They all knew about it, anyway.

"Do you think I'm broken?" I blurted.

Eva lowered her fork. "What are you talking about?"

"I keep having these episodes where my magic seems to kick in, but then it just fizzles out." At least it wasn't the other way round, deserting me right when I needed it most, but still, it wasn't normal. I'd been around enough trainee witches here at Misfits to know that. "What if I'm broken somehow? Flawed, somehow. Like my brother. Only with me, it's my magic that's affected."

I ducked my head, embarrassed by my admission.

"Not a chance." She shook her head. "Your magic is unpredictable, but you know it's there. You've felt it in class. You just need to keep practicing. You'll figure it out, I know you will."

"But it doesn't feel that way. I'm just sitting, spinning my wheels."

"It will click. You've had a lot less time interacting with your unique magic."

"You sound like Glover," I grumbled.

"Maybe she's got a point."

I took a bite of my toast and studied the other occupants of the room. Some were ushering their somewhat sobered up friends back to the privacy of their rooms, and others looked like they'd given up on the pretence of life. On the opposite side of the room, I spotted Reggie, the guy who kept jumping up to defend me whenever Celine went on the warpath. Guilt lanced through me.

"Did he show up last night?" I jutted my chin in his direction.

Eva glanced over at him and then turned back to me. "For a bit, I think. Honestly, he looked kind of lonely."

"He asked me to go with him. I turned him down," I admitted around another bite of food.

"He seems like a nice enough guy," she said.

"Well, it would have been awkward if I'd made it," I said.

She cocked her head to the side. "Why?"

I set the crust of toast down. "Oh, come on, you can't tell me you didn't have a druid-shaped surprise waiting for me."

"What makes you think I had any better resources to find him than you did?"

"You're resourceful," I replied.

"Well, I'll have you know that much to my dismay, there was no such surprise waiting for you. If there had been, do you think he wouldn't have realised something was wrong and come to help?" Her tone was teasing, but then her face grew serious and the skin around her lips pinched.

"Stop blaming yourself. You didn't do anything wrong." I eyed my would-be date across the room. If Zachary wasn't in the picture—I didn't want to get my hopes up that Kelsey would be able to track him down— maybe I should give him a shot. Eva was right. He *did* seem like a nice enough guy.

He looked up from his mug, and I offered a small wave. He smiled at me but didn't make any attempt to approach. The thought of engaging with someone, especially one who seemed to care about me, was too daunting and so I, too, stayed seated.

"Do you think everyone knows what happened last night?" I pushed a tomato around my plate half-heartedly.

"The people who weren't plastered by that point knew something went down. I heard a few people say it was weird Celine wasn't at the party."

"Great," I grumbled. I grabbed my empty mug and was about to head over to the machine for a refill when I caught movement from Celine's table. Miranda slipped out of her seat and approached the coffee machine. It was the only coffee machine in the room—since electricity was moot around this much magic, it had to be magically powered, and I guess the academy's budget didn't stretch to more than one. I toyed with the idea of waiting for her to finish before I went over, but that somewhat went against my whole new not-hiding attitude. I swallowed a sigh and pushed myself to my feet, slowing strolling towards the machine—because I didn't need her thinking I was sneaking up on her and throwing a hot cup of coffee in my face. I really had seen enough of the healers for one week.

I hung a few steps back while Miranda tapped a few

buttons on the machine and thrust her cup under the nozzle.

She let out a strangled scream and yanked her hand away, clutching it to her chest. Her empty cup tumbled to the floor and, with a loud crash, shattered into a hundred pieces.

Her lip trembled, and I could make out half a dozen red blisters forming on her hand. She shoved past me, running back to Jessa with huge crocodile tears streaming down her face.

Jessa and Celine wrapped their arms around her and ushered her from the room, presumably heading for the med wing. I watched them go with a mental shrug.

Too bad. Couldn't have happened to a nicer person.

I stepped round the shattered pieces and set my cup on the machine.

Chapter Eleven

By mid-November, it seemed everyone had lost interest in Celine and her drama. At the very least, she had lost interest in tormenting me for the time being and I could just focus on my work. I sat in Runes class and Rathbone stood at the front of the room. It was a mix of students pulled from across my year, rather than the usual group—not everyone had been assigned to this class. At least Celine and her friends weren't in this lesson, and as usual, most of the class just ignored me.

"Today, we're going to test your translation skills," Rathbone announced.

Groans went up around the room. Runes were literally learning another language, but much to my surprise, it had come somewhat easily to me. I enjoyed deciphering the images and piecing them together to make new words and spells. Or I would once he actually let us cast anything. So far, all we'd been learning was what the different runes meant. Casting magic on a badly drawn or mistranslated rune could have dangerous results, and apparently Rathbone wasn't in a hurry to risk someone wiping out a quarter of the second year with a dodgy spell.

The instructor tapped the board behind him. "I'm

going to give you the first half of our lesson to translate these runes, and then we'll go through and find out how many of you got them correct."

As he settled down behind his desk, I caught sight of Reggie dutifully jotting down the assignment. He, too, had backed off since Halloween. He'd seemed to have gotten shier, in fact. It was hard to imagine any way that it wasn't my fault—I'd done a terrible job of letting him down, and I'd made zero effort to be friendly to him after. In part because I didn't want to lead him on or give him the wrong idea… but maybe I should have given him a little more credit. Some guys were actually capable of being friends with a girl and not expecting more, and he seemed like one of the decent ones. Just because I didn't have any romantic designs on him—and after much soul searching, I was more convinced than ever that I didn't want a relationship with anyone who wasn't Zachary, even if it meant resigning myself to being single—didn't mean I couldn't be friends with him. After all, he'd been there to have my back with Celine on more than one occasion. I would make sure that things between us were good after class. I owed him that much, at the very least.

Turning my attention to the assignment at hand, I took down the string of characters, careful to ensure my penwork was precise. Rathbone's obsessive perfectionism and paranoia had done more for my penmanship than a whole succession of schoolteachers.

All around me, I heard people flipping through the pages of their textbooks, trying to find the answers. Normally, I'd be amongst them—certainly in any other subject here at Braeseth. I was usually the first to need to look up answers. But runes were different. For some reason, they came easily to me, and had ever since my first lesson. The English translations just seemed to stick in my head. Figured. I was a misfit even amongst misfits. Not that I was complaining about it this time. It felt good to excel at something. I jotted down the runes' meanings without hesitation.

"This is too hard," the girl in front of me complained loudly.

"It's not like he's making you do it from memory," I muttered.

The words slipped out of my mouth before I realised I'd spoken. I held my breath, hoping she hadn't heard it and wondering what the hell was wrong with my big mouth. And then she turned in her seat and glared at me.

"We can't all be like you," she said, waving her hand at my lack of textbook. "Just because you've found one non-magical task you're not completely shit at doesn't make you better than the rest of us." Her mouth twisted into a derisive sneer. "Or even as good as us, so don't start getting ideas."

I bit down hard on my tongue to keep quiet. Engaging with her would only result in the tentative peace I'd somehow brokered in this class being smashed to pieces. And I'd been out of line saying what I did—just because she was complaining about something I found easy didn't give me the right to rub her nose in it. And if she hadn't been such a bitch about it, I'd have apologised. Maybe I should just swallow my pride and do it anyway.

"This task doesn't call for collaboration," Rathbone said from behind his desk, and motioned for the girl in front of me to turn back around in her seat, sparing me making the decision.

I could feel my shadow magic slipping along my body from the inside, longing to be free; to teach her that she should show some respect for me. I sucked in a deep breath and blew it out slowly, tamping down on my magic before it could escape. I didn't *want* her to show me some respect. I wanted her to go back to ignoring me.

I felt my magic withdrawing inside me and turned my attention back to the runes in front of me.

As I finished the translation, I read back over my work and couldn't help but smile at what it spelled out. I didn't need to check the answers to know they were right: Rathbone'd had us translate what essentially came out as instructions on how to cast our first rune, followed by the runes *Isa*, which roughly translated as 'patience', or 'block current action', and *thurisaz*: 'hardship', or 'pain'. Or, to give them a little context, don't follow the instructions or he was going to kick our arses. I stifled a chuckle.

The way he'd structured the runes meant that they wouldn't actually do anything if anyone tried to use the specific string of symbols, either. It was rather clever.

The air around me was thick with frustration by the time we reached the midpoint of the lesson. I was the only one who'd stopped working and I slumped down in my chair. I meant what I'd said before about not hiding anymore, but that didn't mean I wanted to draw attention to myself for being the class swot—more than I already had by getting into that dumb argument, that was.

"All right, I think you've all had enough time to translate," Rathbone announced. A few students around me jumped at his words.

Across the room, Reggie sat up straighter, pen poised to correct his answers as we went. I tried to catch his eye and give him a reassuring smile, but he wouldn't meet my gaze. I had some serious bridge mending to do in that direction. Once I survived this lesson.

Please don't let Rathbone call on me.

I didn't want to add any more fuel to that particular blaze. I still hadn't worked out if Rathbone was actually psychic, or if he was just way more perceptive than most of our instructors, but either way he seemed to get the message and left me in peace.

I made small tick marks for each rune I got correct—all of them by the end of the string—in silence. I tried to hide my success by making some disappointed sounds and hanging my head. By the time the lesson was done, I was starting to believe my own disappointment. I just hoped the rest of the class was as easily convinced.

"For those of you who did not get all of today's translation correct, please revise the material and prepare a brief essay on why you believe you were unable to translate accurately. Those of you who were successful, there is a chapter at the end of the text with some additional examples. Prepare those for our next lesson."

Given the level of frustrated grumbling around me, I knew most of the class would be writing those self-reflective essays. For a brief moment I considered writing some flimsy essay to make people think I was a failure, too, but I knew Rathbone would never accept it, and deep down, a tiny part of me was proud that I'd got it right. It was just a dumb translation, but I'd managed it, and that wasn't nothing. Students began filtering out of the room and I slid out of my seat, approaching Reggie as he stowed his book in his bag.

"Pretty tough assignment, huh?" I said.

He shrugged one shoulder. "I missed a couple. Guess I'll be writing that essay." He zipped his bag, still not looking at me.

"Yeah, same."

That caught his attention and he looked at me. His eyes were bright with disbelief. "No, you didn't. We both know this is your best subject, Norah."

I caught myself before I did something really dumb like asking if he paid attention to how I fared in all my classes. Being defensive was not the way to build bridges. Besides, it was pretty common knowledge I was rubbish at most things. "Is it weird I wish I wasn't so good?"

He shook his head. "This place can be messed up like that. You get targeted for being good at things. Sort of makes it tough to excel."

"I could tutor you, if you want. Just in runes, obviously. Like you said, I'm pretty bad at everything else. I'm almost certain if I could be barred from a botany lab, I would be."

His cheeks darkened with a blush. "That's really nice of you. I only got a couple wrong. I think I've just been stressed. But if I'm still having trouble when we actually start casting, I'll let you know."

"Right, yeah. That makes sense," I said. The disappointment that washed over me caught me completely off guard. He'd been so keen to come to my defence before that I'd kind of counted him on my team. It stung that he didn't want to spend time with me.

I looked up from staring at my own feet long enough to catch him looking over my shoulder. I turned to follow his gaze—it was the girl who'd had a go at me during the lesson. She was with a couple of other girls whose names I probably knew if I put my mind to it. They were all fairly pretty. I could see why they'd caught Reggie's attention. I guess he'd lost interest in me after I turned him down for the dance. I mean, that wasn't a bad thing, right? I'd wanted him to move on. Just not to her. I suppose it could have been worse. At least it wasn't Celine.

"I'll see you around," I said and stepped out of his way.

"See you around, Norah," he said with a small smile before he shouldered his bag and headed out the door, right past the girl he'd been eying.

I watched him go. I wanted to wait for the rest of the class to leave before I headed out. I didn't like being in the rushing crowds of students moving from class to class in the corridors.

"I hope you weren't offended I didn't call on you today," Rathbone said.

I didn't turn to face him as I spoke. "It was fine."

"I'm happy to check your answers for you."

"No need. I got them all correct. I liked what you did with it, explaining what we'd be doing when we start casting them. It was kind of poetic."

Rathbone chuckled. "I'm glad someone appreciated my work."

"You didn't have to intervene earlier," I said. *But I'm glad you did.*

"You may think you aren't worth defending, Norah, but you're so very wrong about that. You've got such tremendous potential if you'd just let yourself believe in it. You've been doing amazing things in this class."

"And yet I still can't make my magic work reliably," I reminded him.

"And you think everyone else gets it right all the time?" he said with a snort. "Not even us instructors are perfect, you know."

He had a point. No one was perfect. But he at least understood what made his magic work the way it did. "This is the part where you tell me to just keep trying because I'm still learning, right?"

"I know, the usual instructor spiel. But it's true. And I know it's a cliché, but if you do need to talk, I'm here. So is Instructor Glover. You've got people who have your back, Norah."

"I'll try to remember it," I said, and walked away. I headed out into the corridor. The trio of girls who'd caught Reggie's eye were a few paces ahead of me as I scanned the faces for Eva. We'd planned to spend our free period outside under our tree. I wanted to make the most of it while the weather held—I knew from last year that in a few weeks, the whole area would be a bog.

"How was Runes?"

I jumped half out of my skin and turned to face my best friend with a mock glare.

"You did that on purpose."

"Maybe." She shrugged with a grin, although how anyone could come out of an advanced botany lesson looking that chipper was completely beyond me. In fact, it was beyond me why anyone would want to do an advance botany lesson at all. Way too much time around plants that were way too easy to kill.

"Could have been worse," I said as we made our way to where the corridor branched off to the stairs. "I mean, no-one tried to kill me so it was kinda boring, but I got all the translations right so I'm pretty sure I made at least one new enemy for next week."

"You deserve to be good at something, Nor."

"I guess," I said with a shrug.

"Don't sell yourself short. What'd you learn, anyway? Runes always seemed so complex and confusing to me."

"We just had to translate some runes. It was actually kind of amusing. Rathbone arranged them so they explained what we'd be doing next year in casting them." The words tumbled out of me as I realised just how excited the topic made me.

"She was being such a show-off." I recognised my new definitely-not-friend's voice as it carried easily down the hall to us. "Didn't even bother to take her book out and pretend she didn't know the answers."

I craned my neck to see who she was talking to, but I didn't recognise the cluster of students around her. I spotted Reggie down the hall. Maybe he was working up the courage to approach her. I took a moment to assess her. She really was quite pretty, perfectly made-up face, with a figured that somehow managed to look feminine even in these awful uniforms. It wasn't hard to see why she'd caught Reggie's eye. It would be utterly ridiculous to feel betrayed that he'd show an interest in someone just because they'd been horrible to me, which didn't stop me feeling it.

"Maybe you should be less insecure," Eva called as we passed.

I tried to shush her and clamped my hand down on her arm and squeezed, but the damage was done. The girl spun on her heel, shooting daggers at us.

"I don't need any help with people hating me," I hissed in my best friend's ear.

"I was just telling the truth," she said with a shrug.

"No one asked you," the girl sneered, "because you're a pair of nobodies."

I tried to hurry along before the situation could get worse but then a loud yelp went up from behind us. Morbid curiosity got the better of me and I turned to see that an angry red rash had broken out all across her arms.

She locked eyes with me.

"You!" she snarled, balling her hands into tight, white-knuckled fists. "You did this!"

Oh, to hell with being the bigger person and not making enemies. That ship had well and truly sailed, anyway. I swallowed my denial and cut her a sweet smile.

"Might want to get those looked at."

Her hands twitched—either with the desire to whack me or the urge to scratch, it was hard to imagine which was stronger right now. It probably wasn't a great idea to stick around long enough to see which one won out. I turned away, and as I did, I noticed something off about one of the rashes near her right wrist. It looked—well, it sounded crazy, but it almost looked like one of the runes we'd had in the lesson today. Trick of the light, probably.

I shook my head, trying to dislodge the thought as Eva and I made our way outside. Maybe her insecurity had manifested in self-inflicted rashes. I had no idea what her unique power was, and like Rathbone had said, no-one here had perfect control of their magic. I probably should feel worse for her about that than I did.

"Am I a bad person for thinking it was sort of justice

that she broke out in hives?" I blurted once we were seated beneath the tree.

"Hardly," Eva said with a snort. "She was being a total bitch."

"And I mean, I kind of felt the same way earlier when Celine's friend burned herself. Like, she deserved it." I stared down at my hands as I made the admission. Was this how things had started out for Micah? He'd believed the druids deserved it.

"She definitely did. Well, I suppose Celine would have deserved it more. It doesn't make you a bad person just because you see that, Norah."

Relief washed over me at her statement. It wasn't that I would ever wish harm on anyone, but still. After what had happened with Micah, it was hard not to second guess myself at every turn, especially when people were getting hurt. I was probably overthinking it. These were just freak coincidences. We were free of crazy druid interference, and no matter how big a game Celine talked, there was no chance she was going to overthrow anyone or disrupt the status quo. I just needed to get a grip.

There weren't any conspiracies looming in these halls.

Chapter Twelve

The guilt I'd been feeling after the girl in Runes had broken out in hives faded quickly as November slipped into December and then into January and the new semester. There had been no more strange occurrences, and the majority of our year had gone back to ignoring me. Everything was starting to feel normal again—right down to the Botany textbook spread across my lap that may as well have been written in ancient Gaelic for all the sense it made to me. My eyes were starting to cross from squinting at it so much. Not my favourite way to spend a rainy Saturday.

"I really don't know how you can understand all of this," I complained as Eva scribbled away in a notebook.

"We both have our strengths. I told you before, it's a lot like maths."

"Yup. That's the problem." I closed the book and tossed it aside.

I'd already done my coursework for the rest of my classes, but my heart wasn't in this one. I'd give it a go later on, but there was no point in trying to force myself to understand and remember all the names of different plants. I mean, honestly, who even still labelled things in Latin these days? I toyed with the idea of making a trip down to the canteen or going for a walk, but I didn't feel like being alone. Also, it was the first week of February. It was freezing outside.

"Give me a few minutes to finish my essay and we can go do something fun," Eva said.

I flopped back on my bed and stared up at the ceiling, letting my thoughts wander. As they had a habit of doing when I least wanted them to, they found their way to Zachary. I hated that I was still pining after him. I hadn't heard a word from Kelsey in months. That meant she'd either had no luck in tracking him down or didn't want to be the bearer of bad news. Either way, it only served to frustrate me. And it wasn't like I had time to be worrying about a guy who had probably moved on months ago. I was halfway to graduation, and I needed to sort out what I wanted to do with myself once that happened, now that the idea that I would actually graduate no longer seemed so foreign to me. I could still hear Bevan's voice in the back of my head urging me to reconsider the chance to study at the druid enforcer academy, but nothing had changed. I refused to be part of the system that ruined my brother's life, and that was so incapable of seeing its many injustices.

"Your bag is vibrating," Eva said in a conversational tone.

I blinked and turned to look at her, waiting for her

words to make sense as they rattled around inside my admittedly distracted head. I was still staring at her when my bag slid off my bed and landed on the floor with a loud thud and skittered across the room until my brain finally caught up. There was only one thing in my bag capable of vibrating like that, and unless you're thinking of a communication stone right now, you need to get your mind out of the gutter.

I scrambled off my bed and pounced on it, pausing long enough to thank Eva before scurrying off to the loo. It seemed like a ridiculous place to have a conversation, but it wasn't like whoever was calling could see where I was, and besides, if it was Zachary and not Kelsey on the other end of the stone, answering in front of Eva would just embarrass all three of us.

"Uh, hello?" I cupped the stone in my palms as I sat awkwardly on the toilet, fully clothed.

"Norah, is now a bad time?" Kelsey's voice came through, bouncing off the walls.

"Uh, no, it's a great time," I replied. She *couldn't* see where I was, right? I squinted at the stone suspiciously.

"I know it's been a while, but I wanted to let you know that I found something about your druid friend. If you still want to know, that is. I know it was ages ago you asked about him."

My mouth went dry, and I forgot to breathe for a

moment. She'd actually found something. Maybe the universe had decided I deserved a little good news. *Unless he doesn't want anything to do with you*, my mind reminded me. Worse, maybe he was in trouble. Or hurt. Or sick. Or—

"You did?" My voice trembled with trepidation.

"I'm sorry it took so long for me to track him down, but he's been on an assignment out of the country. He hasn't long been back."

My heart hammered in my chest. He was okay. He'd been away and probably out of communication with anyone he'd have wanted to talk to. He wasn't ignoring me after all.

"That's great. I mean that he's back. Not that he was away and everything. Or maybe that was a good thing. Um, I'll shut up now."

Kelsey's laughter echoed in the room around me, and I wished the stone had a volume control. "I've let him know you were trying to get in touch with him and he said he appreciated the message."

My excitement turned to stone in my chest. "That's it? Not that he'd get in touch?" *Or that he missed me?*

"It was a brief connection. I'm sure he'll be in touch now that he's back in the same time zone. How are things going otherwise?"

"Fine, I guess. Just trying to keep up with classes and

not get caught up in the drama of the rest of the students."

"You'll make it through. You're more resilient than you think." There was a long pause and then she said, "I'm sorry, I need to go. I just thought you'd want to know."

I wanted to ask what she possibly needed to go do on a Saturday but held my tongue. She worked for the Circle, and they didn't operate on a strict weekday schedule. "Thanks for that. I really do appreciate it."

The stone died down and I sat there staring at it. So, Zachary was around and might be reaching out. I couldn't even begin to pretend I wasn't excited about the prospect. On the other hand, he hadn't reached out already, and he'd been back long enough for Kelsey to find out, so I was probably getting my hopes up for nothing.

I retreated to the dorm to find Eva lounging on her bed. "So, your druid boyfriend's back?"

"You weren't supposed to hear that," I said.

"These walls are remarkably thin," she said with a smirk. "Don't start losing your mind waiting for him to get in touch."

"Easier said than done," I said, not quite keeping the irritation from my voice. So much for not being the type to run around pining after guys.

She kicked her legs over the side of the bed and stood

up. Before I could do more than raise an eyebrow, she grabbed my hand and dragged me out of the room.

"Where are we going?"

"Some other students are doing a study group for spellcraft and I said I'd go," she said.

"And that means I have to go too because…?"

"Because you could use the practice, too."

Ouch. But she wasn't wrong, and it wasn't like the rest of the class didn't already know I sucked at most courses. And who knew, being around other people might help. Well, probably not, but it didn't hurt to find out. And being in a setting without the pressure to perform and impress an instructor had to make it easier. As long as…

"They won't mind, right? I mean, I'm not exactly flavour of the month."

Eva rolled her eyes. "I keep telling you, Nor, not everyone round here hates you. Time you found that out for yourself."

I expected Eva to lead me to the library and one of the few rooms that littered the upper floor where the third-year students often congregated. I wasn't entirely sure what they studied up there, but I did know it didn't pay to interrupt someone if they were casting spells. Backlash could be dangerous. Deadly, even, if the spell was powerful enough. The academy took the danger seriously enough that it was strictly prohibited to go into one of the rooms when they were in use, or even knock on the door.

But she didn't lead me to the library, instead moving through the corridors until we reached a row of lecture rooms, and then into the spellcrafting lab. The room was empty, but a tray of amulets sat on the instructor's desk.

"We aren't studying in here, are we?" The question hung in the empty air between us, echoing back at us off the walls.

"No, but the instructor said we could borrow some amulets for practice," she said, and scooped up the contents of the tray.

It turned out we were headed for one of those upper rooms and it was crammed with more people than feasible. I spotted Rory and Reggie sitting on opposite sides of the cramped space. Rory met my gaze and I offered him a small smile. We'd had that moment together during last semester checking grades and I'd seen there was a kindness beneath his rough exterior. He hadn't said much to me this semester at all. Then again, it wasn't like I'd gone out of my way to talk to him, either. I spotted a dark-haired girl sitting next to him. Sophia. Come to think of it, I'd seen them together a lot this year. Maybe they were dating. I caught sight of their entwined hands. Yup, definitely dating. I guess he'd been kind of busy with his own drama.

Unfortunately, the only spots available in the room were right at the front, which I assumed was kept free for Eva who'd organised the session, and the other spot right beside Rory. So I squeezed my way around the perimeter to sit beside him.

"Surprised to see you here," I whispered, trying to make conversation.

"Why?" he muttered out of one corner of his mouth.

"I just thought you were doing well in this class," I answered.

He shrugged. "I could use a refresher."

Sophia leaned round him to scowl at me.

"Look, I don't know what you're trying to prove, but maybe just don't talk to us," she said. "Rory's not interested in you."

I opened my mouth to tell her it wasn't like that—I wasn't interested in Rory, and even if I had been, I'd never make a move on someone who was in a relationship—but she turned away with a swish of her long hair.

Rory shot me an apologetic smile, and I thought I saw a crinkle of embarrassment around his eyes before he shifted in his seat to focus his attention on his girlfriend.

Across the room, I caught Reggie watching us. I inclined my head toward to him to let him know I saw him watching and he got a sheepish grin on his face. It disappeared, replaced by a look of concentration as Eva passed out the amulets.

"Uh, so I know I'm no instructor, but I figured it would be good to get a study group together since this is kind of a tough subject," she said, shifting her weight from side to side as her hands clamped onto the back of the chair in front of her. "Maybe we should work in pairs?"

There was a murmur of agreement and I realised too late that there was no way I would be able to pair up with Eva. A redhead girl whose name was Amanda scooted her chair beside my roommate. I thought about Reggie and hesitated—I didn't want him to think I was pushing him to spend time with me—and by the time I decided it didn't matter, it was too late. He'd already paired up with someone else. I looked around the room and realised *everyone* had paired up. We were an odd number. Worse, most of them had already started working, and I didn't want to interrupt anyone's focus. Beside me, Rory and Sophia were engaged in a hushed conversation. But they seemed to be the only ones not working. Great.

I swallowed my embarrassment and turned to them, focusing my attention on Sophia rather than Rory, because I really didn't want her to think I was trying to move in on her man. I didn't want him to think that, either, come to it—my interests were elsewhere.

"Uh, everyone's paired up. Do you mind if I work with you two?"

Her scowl deepened, and I caught Rory squeezing her hand. She sucked in a deep breath and forced a smile that was as fake as my love for botany.

"Sure."

Well, she hadn't told me to get lost, which I figured was as close to a win as I was going to get. And, honestly, a whole lot better than I'd expected. Maybe Eva was right. Not everyone round here hated me. I mean, disliked, sure, I was definitely getting that vibe from Sophia right now, but I could understand that. She'd soon realise I wasn't interested in Rory that way. With a small smile and the fluttering of hope in my chest, I turned my attention to the amulet.

The stone was clear, which meant it was waiting for a spell to be cast on it. It was set into a metal disc with tiny runes delicately etched into it. We'd been taught that these were a standard set of runes meant to amplify and contain the power we imbued in the amulet. I recognised them from my lessons with Rathbone. I spotted the runes for control, confinement, and amplification.

"So, I think we start with adding magic to the amulet, right?" I tried to frame it so I didn't come across as a know-it-all. I was close enough to getting that reputation in Runes without adding to it.

"Yeah, I guess," Rory said, hesitating as he picked up his amulet. It looked so tiny in his beefy grip.

Sophia picked up hers, too, and I could sense her focus crackling in the air around us. As the long seconds passed, nothing happened. Her face was screwed up in a mix of concentration and frustration, and I bit back the urge to suggest she try doing it differently. It wasn't like I knew she was doing it wrong, and I doubted I could do any better. *Could I?* I hadn't been very successful in trying to craft spells in class, but maybe… maybe that was because I hadn't been paying attention to the engraved runes. Knowing what they did now made it easier to not be afraid that I was going to lose control. They were built in safeguards to make sure we didn't add too much magic. My magic wasn't going to hurt anyone. *I* wasn't going to hurt anyone.

I held the amulet in my right hand and let the tip of my left index finger trace the runes, stopping on the one for confinement. I wanted the magic to stay within the amulet. My shadows seemed to snap to attention as I felt the texture of the rune against the pad of my finger. It wanted to be used and to obey. That was… new. From the corner of my eye I saw movement as Sophia dumped her amulet down and Rory picked up his, but I shut them both out and focused on the sensation of my magic inside me, primed and ready to use.

I let it out. Just enough to turn the stone from clear to smoky. Magic swirled inside the amulet stone, and I studied it. The confine rune seemed to glow slightly as the light played across it.

So that's how it works.

That seemed far easier than I'd ever thought it would be. Maybe I wasn't totally rubbish at everything after all. Maybe I could find a place for myself deciphering or using runes. When I looked away from the amulet, I realised all eyes had landed on me.

"What?" I blurted.

"I've never seen you do that," Eva said.

"I guess I just finally realised how it all works. It's really thanks to Rory," I said, hoping to give him a bit of an ego boost so he wouldn't feel bad I'd pulled it off when he hadn't. Too late, I realised how that would probably look to Sophia. Dammit.

"Don't look at me. I don't know what the hell I'm doing," he snapped, and slammed his amulet down against the table.

The stone began to vibrate against the table as he pushed away from it. I itched to scoop it up and examine it—if any of the runes had been damaged, they might not function correctly. If he'd put any magic in there and the runes failed it would need to be contained or dissipated, or—

The stone shattered before I could move, spraying dozens of tiny shards all over Rory's chest and upper arms. It somehow managed to miss his face entirely, but I could still see the tiny abrasions and burn marks from the residual magic the amulet had stored.

"Rory!" Sophia screamed.

Panic and acid guilt clawed at me. I wasn't the one who'd damaged the amulet, but I could have acted faster to contain it, or not said anything about Rory in the first place, and now someone was hurt. And I'd ruined Eva's practice session. She'd convinced the instructor to trust her with the amulets and now she'd have to explain why they were short one and how someone had ended up in the medwing while trying to do a simple practice lesson.

"Stay the hell away from me," Rory snapped in my direction as he stormed out of the room, trying to brush off the stone shards as he went, leaving a trail of dark crimson granules in his wake. Sophia paused long enough to cut me an evil look and then hurried after him. The rest of the group dispersed, leaving their amulets behind until it was just me and Eva left. I helped her gather the amulets and heaved a sigh.

"It was a good idea," I tried to console her, and then gave her a friendly nudge with my shoulder. "And even if you didn't help the rest of them, I think I understand how it works now."

Eva snorted and shook her head.

"Then maybe you should be the one leading the study sessions. I'm clearly terrible at it. It barely lasted twenty minutes and someone got hurt on my watch."

"You are not terrible. Rory just has a temper. Everyone knows that. I'm sure he'll be fine. And his pride will survive, too. He probably just didn't like looking bad in front of Sophia."

Which was my fault, not Eva's. I swallowed. No-one ever warned me building bridges was this hard. Maybe I should stick to the ones I'd already built.

As we headed back down to the spellcrafting lab to return the remaining amulets and turn in the broken one for containment, the idea grew on me. Zachary was back and I was going to make it my mission to see him, even if it ended up souring everything we'd had last year. Because given everything I'd been through, how bad could it possibly be?

Chapter Thirteen

I couldn't hide my good mood as I settled into my seat in Energy Manipulation. I'd *finally* made contact with Zachary, and he was actually interested in seeing me off academy grounds. The fact we'd finally connected filled me with hope as winter turned into spring, and the promise of new life filled the academy gardens—so long as I wasn't the one to tend them.

"Careful, people night notice you look happy," Eva whispered as she settled in beside me.

"Let them see. I don't care," I said, completely unable to smother the smile spreading across my face. "I *am* happy."

The door opened and Celine stalked in, giving me a disapproving glare as she marched to an empty seat one row over. She'd been leaving me alone, too. Without having to worry about being magically jumped in the corridors, I'd been able to study, and I was doing halfway decent in a few classes now. Runes was still my best subject, but I was starting to get the hang of Energy Manipulation and Spellcraft. At least half the class were speaking to me—Eva had been right about that, and ten kinds of smug when I acknowledged it—and even those who weren't mostly just followed Celine's lead and left me in peace. It really had been a great few weeks. Of course, I'd written off botany as a lost cause, no matter what Eva said.

I caught sight of Reggie entering the room and he made a beeline for the seat in front of me. He hadn't been around as much lately, but we still sometimes exchanged friendly looks from across the canteen.

He pivoted in his seat to face me. "So, what do you think Rathbone's going to have us doing today?"

"Uh, not sure," I answered, caught off guard by the sudden intrusion in my conversation with Eva.

"I heard some of the third years talking about this really wicked defensive magic lesson he teaches before the end of semester. I hope it's today."

"That would be cool," I agreed, feeling awkward and groping for words.

"I know you think you aren't good at stuff, but you are," he said, smiling and nodding in what was probably supposed to have been an encouraging way.

Rathbone's appearance in the lecture room's doorway spared me from trying to find an appropriate response to the unexpected compliment, and as he closed the door and strode to his desk, Reggie turned back around to face the front of the room. Across the room, Celine continued to glare at me; like my happiness was somehow offensive to her. Well, that was not my problem, and I was not going to let it spoil my good mood.

"I know I don't need to remind you all that we are only four weeks away from exams," Rathbone announced, eliciting grumbling from around the room.

He waved his hands for quiet. "We all knew this time was coming. And today's lesson will be the culmination of what we've been working toward," he said and began pacing in front of his desk. "By now, you've mastered the ability to create energy balls and can direct them with limited accuracy."

He glanced Rory's direction as he spoke and earned a few chuckles. I could still see the spot on the opposite wall where he'd gone off the mark and singed the décor. Rory ducked his head and managed to make his bulky frame shrink some under the attention from the rest of the class.

"Today, you're going to be pairing off and practicing turning your energy balls into shields to deflect your partner's attack," Rathbone continued.

The way Reggie sat up a little straighter in his seat suggested this was the lesson he'd been hoping for. It would have been a useful skill last year when I was trying to stop the druids from stealing all of our magic. Maybe someone should speak to the dean about updating the syllabus—you know, and putting defensive magic first. Not that I could have used it last year. I'd gotten lucky sustaining an energy ball for a minute during exams. I turned to Eva, ready to pair off, when Rathbone spoke again.

"You're going to be partnering down the rows," he said, gesturing first forward and then backward, meaning the first two seats were paired and the back two seats were paired.

That meant I was partnered with Reggie. I fixed Eva with a sad look and a shrug—we rarely got to work together in lessons anymore—and turned my attention to the guy in front of me. Reggie's eyes were alight when he turned his chair to face me.

"You can go first," he said, his face beaming with a dopey grin.

"Uh, I'm not sure how you even make a shield. You sounded like you had a better idea of how it all works. You should go first."

He tilted his head to one side for a moment, contemplating my statement before he nodded in agreement. "I don't think you'll need me to show you, but if it makes you more comfortable. Just go easy on me."

There was more chance of my energy ball fizzling out of creation than there was of it actually doing any damage to him, but I kept that observation to myself and let him have his excitement. We moved the chairs and desk out of the way so there was room to manoeuvre and as we did, I spotted the tiny runes on the floor, spaced out at even intervals. I recognised them from class. They were fail-safes in case things went horribly wrong. They were meant to contain energy and siphon it away, which seemed like a smart move given what we were about to do. It'd save the healers having to work overtime, if nothing else.

I watched as Reggie's brow furrowed in concentration. He held his hands out in front of him and the air grew thick with the scent of ozone. Energy crackled along his fingers and jumped from one hand to the other, forming a bridge that spider-webbed out until it formed a perfect sphere. It was a fiery mix of yellows and oranges. I frowned. I'd never seen one like that before. It even got Rathbone's attention.

"Keep that focus in check," he said, before moving along to watch other students.

Some part of me knew I should be trying to create my own energy ball to throw at him, but all I could do was sit transfixed as his bright ball of electricity formed between his fingers. Slowly, he eased his hands apart. The energy followed his motion and the ball flattened out into a disc shape.

"That's brilliant," I breathed.

"It's only brilliant if it holds up," he said. "Come on, show me what you can do, Norah."

I stood still, a foot away from him, and tried not to panic. I could do this. It didn't have to be perfect. That wasn't the point of the lesson. And yet I couldn't shake the feeling that everyone else was watching me, judging me. It had been nearly a year since everything happened and I still heard the whispers behind my back. Still felt the glances as I walked the corridors.

Turning to my left, I watched as Eva pulled her hands apart, elongating her sphere into a disc like Reggie had done. Her head snapped up and her arms moved in slow motion as her partner lobbed an energy ball at her. My breath caught in my throat. It struck her shield and the energy crackled along the surface of her spell, starting to eat away at her magic. I could see Eva's lips press into a thin line of determination and focus as she poured all of herself into diffusing the attack. Finally, after what felt like minutes, she managed to deflect the rest of the energy ball into the floor. The runes around her feet glowed with a faint purple hue as they absorbed the displaced magic.

I nodded and turned back to Reggie. I could do this. I flexed my hands and turned my attention inward, letting my body focus on connecting with my magic. It was easier than it had been last year. Easier than it had been a couple of months ago, even. I took a slow, steadying breath and opened my eyes. The energy swirling between my hands was inky, like a violent storm cloud ready to unleash hell. It was more shadow than energy, but no-one was going to be judging that.

"Come on, what are you waiting for?" Reggie said, one corner of his lip quirking up into a teasing smile.

"Don't rush me," I hedged, rolling the ball from one hand to the other. I didn't want to give him too much warning. I wanted to see if he could anticipate my move and block the attack. And I didn't want to get my ball stuck to my hand while anyone was watching.

"Any time now," he said, an edge seeping into his tone.

Across the room, I caught Celine bouncing an energy ball in her hand like she was ready to lob it overarm. "Norah can't even do a simple assignment without losing control," she said, her voice carrying easily above the silence of everyone's focus.

Reggie's head snapped to attention in her direction, and for a moment I thought he was going to come to my defence again—just when Celine had laid off giving me a hard time about it. I opened my mouth to stop him, and my control flickered. The ball flew from my hands, straight at Reggie. I tried to warn him, but he was with it enough to turn back and throw up his hands to block my attack. Unlike when Eva had caught her partner's energy ball, mine consumed his shield in shadow in seconds. I could see beads of sweat popping out along his hairline as he shook the magic off his hands, casting it down into the floor to be absorbed by the protection runes.

"I'm so sorry," I said, closing the distance between us.

"You don't have to apologise. You did exactly what was supposed to happen," he answered, still glancing at Celine. She gave him an exaggerated shrug.

"Don't let her bother you," I said, hoping I sounded less bothered than I was by her taunts. I lifted one shoulder in a shrug. "I don't."

"You saved her, and everyone else in this academy. She should be grateful."

Much as I agreed, I didn't want to rehash history. I just wanted to make it through class without undoing all my hard work of the last few months.

"Well, at least I've got you," I said.

His cheeks burned pink with embarrassment at my words. I hadn't meant them in any sort of romantic sense, and I really hoped he hadn't taken it that way. My mind was definitely focused on seeing Zachary again. On kissing him again. But I wanted Reggie to know I appreciated the fact he treated me like a human being, and had done even when everyone else was still hating on me.

"Anyway, I think I've got the idea of it now. Want to switch roles?"

He nodded and wiped his palms on the front of his

trousers, as if drying them off. Maybe I'd made him nervous with my comment. I shouldn't have said anything. I'd made it weird and now it was all he was going to think about.

…And apparently he wasn't the only one. Besides, he was probably just sweating from the effort of defending my rogue not-quite-energy ball.

Focus, Norah.

I tried to centre myself again, to pull the magic from within me and imagine it elongating into a shield in front of me before Reggie could burn me to a crisp with an energy ball. The world around me dimmed as the shadows took hold, guiding my magic. They swirled and undulated down my arms as I willed the energy to coalesce in my palms. The shadows wrapped around my fingers, lacing together in an intricate latticework, devoid of any electrical current. This was all darkness, ready to consume anything that crossed its path.

No, this isn't what I need.

I needed electricity. I needed to do the bloody assignment the way Rathbone wanted it. There was no way I should still be this out of control of my own damned powers. Despite my internal protests, my magic continued to tighten into a dark sphere in my hands. I sensed other people's gazes on me, but there was nothing I could do to stop them. They were as stuck in this bizarre tableau as I was.

Across from me, Reggie's electricity burned bright orange and white against my shadow. My power longed to snuff his out and if he let go, I had no doubt that's what would happen. *Please, just let this be energy.* Where the shadows had been silky and featherlight before, they became coarse, abrasive. They were fighting me, and every breath made them *hurt*.

The haze around me began to lift as a new sensation took over. White hot paint racing from the tips of my fingers up toward my elbows. I looked down to see my hands were on fire. Literal fire. Out of the corner of my eye I saw Celine blowing out a zap of energy and mouthing 'Oops'.

"Norah, you need to direct the magic down to the ground," Rathbone said, stepping up beside me.

I wanted to. I wanted to follow his instruction with every fibre of my being, but that being was no longer listening to me. I grit my teeth, refusing to cry out in agony in front of everyone. Celine had done something to cause this, she had to have. And the look of pure fury on Reggie's face, framed by the still-swirling corona of his energy ball, told me that I was right.

"Norah, you can do this," Eva said from my left.

I latched on to her voice and pictured what she'd done to disperse the magic earlier. I forced my arms downward and, with as much control as I could muster, pushed the magic out of me. In painstaking slow motion, the shadows and fire descended toward the floor. The runes around my feet lit up and I could practically see their magic reaching up to consume mine.

I couldn't look at my hands as the magic faded from my skin. I didn't want to see the burned mess they'd become. But I needed to know what sort of damage I was working with. Everything below the elbow felt numb, which couldn't be good. Burn injuries that came with lack of feeling were usually bad.

I sucked up my courage and squeezed one eye open. Relief forced the breath out of me in a loud whoosh. My arms were blistered, but no worse than they'd been back on Halloween.

"Let me see," Rathbone said, his voice reassuringly calm, though the worst of my panic had already faded. It hurt, but I'd had worse. Also from Celine. This was getting out of hand.

Rathbone steered me into a seat, then crouched down beside me to inspect my arms.

"You'll be fine. The healers will have you fixed up in no time."

He rose to his feet again and rounded on Celine.

"What happened?" he demanded.

"I'm sorry, Instructor Rathbone," Celine said, her

face the picture of contrition. "I lost control.

"That had better be the truth."

He turned his attention back to me, and over his shoulder I caught Celine snickering with Jessa and Miranda, and miming crying faces. But I wasn't going to cry. Hell, no. I was going to kick her arse.

"Where do you think you're going?" Rathbone asked, and I realised I was on my feet. I shook my head and my shoulders slumped.

"Nowhere."

"Good. But since you're on your feet, I suggest you head over to the infirmary and get the healers to take a look. Eva will go with you."

"I don't need an escort."

"Eva will go with you," Rathbone repeated, and I clamped my jaw shut. I had enough enemies round here without making one of Rathbone.

I fell into step with my friend and headed out of the room, taking care not to touch my arms to anything.

Behind me, I heard Rathbone dismiss the class and ask Celine to stay behind. I was grateful to be out of his range because the edge in his tone was sharp enough to have left flesh wounds if it were made tangible. Even so, I doubted Celine would face more than just a stern talking to from Bevan. She scared him with how close she'd come to enacting her plan to overthrow him, and everyone knew it.

"I didn't even do anything to her," I growled as Eva steered me toward the infirmary. "Hell, I didn't even say anything when she was running her stupid mouth."

"She's petty and vindictive," she replied, her grip ironclad around my shoulders, and I wasn't sure if she was supporting me, or stopping me doing something dumb—like going back and getting my arse kicked by Celine again. "That's all the excuse she needs to lash out at you or anyone else."

Maybe that was true, but I was getting sick of running around with a target painted on my back. There was nothing I could have done to stop Celine doing what she did.

But I was sure as hell going to find a way to stop her doing it again.

Chapter Fourteen

Losing three days before exams waiting for the healing magic to set after Celine's little stunt was not what I'd hoped for, especially when my arms were healed in one. I was pretty sure this was Rathbone's idea of putting me in protective custody—like I had time to waste on things like that—but Eva had 'helped' me make the most of it by shoving a textbook in front of me at every opportunity. By the time the healers agreed I could leave, there was actually some sort of hope I wasn't going to get an outright fail in botany. But right now, that was the last thing on my mind.

"Are you sure you don't want me to go with you for moral support?" Eva called from the dorm.

I stood in the bathroom studying my reflection and tugged on the hem of the top she'd lent me. One day I was actually going to have to invest in my own wardrobe. Just as soon as people round here stopped trying to kill me, because that was ruining *all* my best clothes.

"No, I don't need you there to chaperone me," I called back, rolling my eyes at my own reflection. "Last time I checked, we weren't in the eighteen hundreds."

"Ah, come on, don't make me say it. I need an excuse to get out of here."

Zachary and I were meeting up at Fantail Market. It wasn't like the place was small—there were plenty of things she could check out without unintentionally interrupting our date. At least, I hoped it was a date.

"Oh. Well in that case, of course you can come," I said, and left the restroom. I found her already dressed to go out, her academy uniform discarded on the floor.

"How are we getting there?" she asked and twisted her long dark locks around one hand.

My stomach lurched. Crap. I hadn't thought about that. There were no non-magical ways to get to the marketplace, and since neither of us could cast a portal, we'd have to beg use of a transportation stone. I hated those bloody things. There hadn't been a time I'd used one and not nearly lost my lunch as a result.

"Yeah, you're definitely coming," I decreed. Glancing down at the outfit I wore now, "Also, I should bring an extra shirt in case our arrival ruins this one."

Eva pursed her lips, took in my apparel, and went in search of something else to match the bottom half. I'd been joking, but actually it seemed like a good idea. I was nervous enough to puke as it was. She stuffed the top into a bag and slung it over her shoulder.

"Let's go."

"Any idea who we can borrow a stone from?"

She grinned and patted her bag. "Lucky for you, I

borrowed one this morning."

We made it to the entry hall without anyone paying us any attention, and we were just about to make our escape off the grounds, and outside of the anti-transport wards, when I heard Glover's voice from behind us.

"Where are you girls off to?" she asked with what sounded more like genuine interest than any sort of suspicion.

"Uh, just the market for a little time away from campus," I answered. She might like me, and I was grateful she'd had my back with Celine, but she didn't need to know the details of my tenuous love life. Plus, I really wasn't ready to admit to anyone I was spending time with druids. Not when it would put a target on my back with the other students, and definitely not when Bevan might take it the wrong way and hassle me about training with them again.

"It's good to get off grounds for a bit now and then," she said, implicitly giving us permission to leave.

It wasn't that second years couldn't leave the grounds, but it was more an unspoken rule that you didn't go off at will until your last year. By then, they assumed you had enough control over your magic not to cause too much chaos and bring trouble down on the academy.

"Well, have a nice day, Instructor," Eva said and tugged at my arm.

We hurried through the front door and emerged into the warm summer air. The bright sunlight temporarily blinded me and I blinked furiously, trying to clear the spots dancing in my vision. I didn't need to trip down the stairs and show up looking like I'd been assaulted.

"Going on a date with your girlfriend?" Celine called in a sing-song voice from across the grounds as we approached the outer limits of the campus. "Or maybe you're just running away because you finally realised no one wants you here."

My hands balled into fists before I could stop them. What was it with her? The only reason I wasn't whacking her in the face right now was because I didn't want to show up on my actual date with bruised knuckles. On the other hand, Zachary knew how to handle himself in a fight; maybe he'd like the warrior princess look.

"Don't engage with her," Eva hissed under her breath.

I wanted to listen to her, really, I did, but it was a low blow, insinuating that there was anything wrong with me being on a date with a girl. Sure, it wasn't true, but that wasn't the point.

I pivoted to look at her.

"What's the matter, Celine—jealous? Because you seem awfully obsessed with me recently. Is that what all your petty little stunts have been about?"

Miranda and Jessa let out "oohs" as if I'd just thrown down some sort of gauntlet. Children, the pair of them. Did they have any idea what they were involved in? Celine glared at me and took a step closer, but I stood my ground. I was done running. She might be able to throw an energy ball at me, but not even she was that stupid to do it with so many witnesses.

"And for your information, we aren't on a date. But even if we were, we wouldn't be asking your permission, because despite what you seem to think, you don't actually have any power around here."

I turned on my heel and marched up to the front gates before she could respond. The wards preventing anyone from coming or going recognised us, and the gates swung open, allowing us to step through.

"You can't just let it go with her, can you?" Eva shook her head and fished the transportation stone from the depths of her bag.

"I couldn't. Not that. I've put up with a lot from her, but there's a line. She's lucky I didn't deck her."

She flashed me a small smile and held out her hand, the stone gripped in the other. "Come on, you've got a real date to get to."

I held my breath and tried not to suffocate as the stone plucked us from the spot near the academy and deposited us half a block from the coffee shop where we'd met up at the end of summer. The street was busy with vendors hawking their goods under makeshift tents and awnings, and clusters of shoppers moving from one to another.

The world righted itself and as expected, my stomach sloshed, and my breakfast threatened to make a reappearance. I let go of Eva's hand and darted behind a large potted plant outside a clothing shop and bent double, waiting for the nausea to pass. At least if Zachary happened upon me in this position, he'd know why. Small mercies and all that.

"You all right, Miss?" a concerned woman with a beehive hairdo called from the front of the shop.

I looked up and met her gaze.

"Brilliant, thanks," I answered, and managed to straighten without any unpleasant consequences, which was frankly more than I'd dared to hope for. The sooner I learned to portal, the better.

I backed away from my little hideaway to find Eva stuffing something back into her bag. I knew she'd been doing extra work this year. She'd said it had something to do with her mum, but she hadn't elaborated, and I'd been so focused on my own stuff I hadn't asked. Some friend I was. I knew it was just the two of them back home. She'd never met her father and after some hiccups along the way—including her manifestation event—she'd stopped looking for him. She was the only one there to look out for her mum, and I was supposed to look out for *her*. I needed to double down on my best friend duties.

"You're supposed to meet him here, right?" She gestured to the coffee shop across the way, snapping me from my thoughts.

"Yeah."

"Okay. Well, I'm going to make myself scarce, then. I'll meet you back here in a few hours."

"All right. See you later."

I gave her a quick one-armed hug and then she melted into the throngs of people moving to and fro on the walkways. I stood there staring up at the coffee shop, gnawing at my lower lip. I could go in and get something for myself while I waited. But if he showed up and I'd already got something, he'd wonder if he was late or how long I'd been sitting there. Or he might not see me outside, and think I'd decided to skip out on him entirely. Maybe then *he'd* skip out, and—

"Norah." Zachary's voice came from my right and I turned slowly, my breath caught in my throat until my eyes came to rest on him. A wave of relief crashed over me as I took in his broad shoulders and rugged face, his lips curved into a boyish smile. He wore regular clothes— a pair of jeans and a shirt—instead of his enforcer uniform, and the sight sent warmth racing to my belly.

His eyes sparkled and a gust of wind—one that I suspected was really his air magic—ruffled his hair as he came towards me, giving him a roguish look.

"I hope you weren't waiting long," he said, his voice that delicious honey baritone that I remembered so well—and my memory hadn't done it justice.

"I just got here," I answered, smoothing the hem of the blouse down, and then catching myself in the act and forcing my hands to still. "Um, do you want to go in?"

"After you," he said and pulled the door open for me.

Whether he'd come expecting to have to pay for my order or not, he waved away my offer and picked up the tab. A few moments later we were sat at a secluded table around the back of the shop sipping coffee and sharing a croissant.

"You look well," I said, and immediately felt my cheeks burn. Seriously. After all this time, 'you look well'? Could I have sounded any more cliché?

"I was going to say the same about you." He took a sip from his mug and set it back on the table. "I'm sorry I didn't get back in touch over summer. I meant to, but with everything that happened last year, I just needed some time to think."

"I get it," I said and stared down at the food between us, which suddenly looked very unappetising. I'd been wrong. This wasn't a date. He regretted what had happened between us and was looking for a way to let me down gently. I swallowed the lump in my throat, and it reformed immediately.

"I know you're mad at me. I've been a crappy friend," he said. Before I could respond, he reached across the table and hooked a finger under my chin, forcing me to look him in the eye. "I'm going to make up for it. I promise."

My mouth went dry, and butterflies erupted in my stomach. I fumbled my mug to my lips in an attempt to wash away the lump from my throat. He pulled his hand away before I spilled the contents everywhere.

I looked around at the shop and couldn't help remembering that conversation back on Valentine's Day last year. Our dream of owning a little coffee and book shop.

"You may be a crappy friend, but you've got a good memory," I said.

He glanced at the facade behind him. "It felt appropriate and like a nice nod to our little secret." He winked and I couldn't help smiling.

"So, how's it been this year?" He set his mug down and turned his attention on me.

"You know, sometimes okay. Sometimes terrible. And exams are just around the corner. I think I'm going to pass everything and avoid being held back." I meant to stop there, but the words kept tumbling out. "Well, okay, so I've sort of written off botany, but Eva insists she's going to get me a passing grade, which I'm pretty sure is going to take a small miracle or a large bribe."

"No more dark and twisted plots to overthrow the status quo, I hope."

"So far, none to be had. Unless you count Celine's latest plot to drive me to distraction. I swear, it's like tormenting me is her sole pleasure in life."

He shook his head with a smile.

"What?" I demanded.

"Did you ever consider that she might be jealous of you and your power?"

I snorted with amusement. "Yeah, right. I can still barely control it most days. She's miles ahead of me there. She's got nothing to be jealous of."

"I don't know. I think you're pretty spectacular. And I'd definitely want you in my corner in a fight."

I let out a laugh. "You can't be serious."

"I seem to recall you saved the day last year."

"I had help. And I didn't know what I was doing."

"You don't give yourself enough credit."

I blushed and glanced down at my hands.

"So, what have you been up to?" Redirecting the conversation seemed easier than fumbling for a response to his words. In my head, I catalogued today in the definite "not a date" category. We were just friends catching up.

"I've been busy helping out at the academy. Nothing big, just offering some extra tutoring for struggling students—not that my old Combat Magic instructor approved. He thinks if someone is struggling it's proof they're not good enough to be there. Fortunately, not everyone agrees with that. And then I was overseas for a bit."

Kelsey had mentioned that. "But you're around more now, right?"

He nodded. "Definitely. And I've arranged to take the next month off. No students to tutor, no assignments to report on."

His smile told me what his words didn't. He was purposely taking time to spend with a certain something. And by all the gods was I praying he meant me. The conversation died down as we finished our drinks. Movement caught my eye through the window, and I spotted Eva outside and blinked in surprise. Had we really been here for two hours? It felt like barely a few minutes.

"Looks like my ride's here," I said.

He stood and offered me his hand. "Still getting nauseous from the stone?"

"It's embarrassing that you even know that."

He passed me a little stick of something that smelled of honey. "Try this. It might help."

I accepted his offering and popped it in my mouth. It dissolved instantly and coated the back of my throat. I exhaled and a tiny plume of honey-scent fog passed over my lips. A cooling sensation spread across the back of my mouth.

"It feels weird," I said.

"Trust me, it will help. It lasts about twenty minutes. Long enough to get you where you're going."

"And you couldn't have told me about it last year?"

"I've got a friend who works in experimental spells and charms," he said. "He came up with it a few weeks back."

"Experimental?" I cocked an eyebrow. "I better not grow a tail."

But if it worked—and I didn't grow any extra appendages—I wasn't going to argue. He held the door open for me and we stepped out into the street. Eva spotted us and waved. I turned to look at Zachary and he leaned in, planting a quick peck on my cheek. My heart fluttered. He *did* feel something for me beyond friendship.

"I'll talk to you soon," he said and looped his arm through mine, escorting me across the street.

"Nice to see you again," he said to Eva.

"You, too."

He gave my hand a quick squeeze. "Safe travels. I hope you have a more pleasant return trip."

I chuckled, which combined with the honey concoction was a strange sensation, and then watched his retreating back as he headed off into the marketplace.

Eva gave me a funny look but I just shook my head, and accepted her hand. The stone hurtled us through nothingness, and a second later, my feet touched down onto solid ground just outside the academy's gates. I stretched out an arm and waited for the nausea to come crashing down on me. And waited. Then my lips spread into a slow smile. Cool.

"I need to stop by the Botany lab for a bit," Eva said, as we headed into the academy. "Catch up with you later?"

We parted ways, and I took my time heading back to the dorm. The smart thing to do would be to revise for exams while I had the time. Even if they were still a few weeks off, I could use all the practice I could get. But I was enjoying the fact that even if it hadn't really been a date, there was the promise of a real one in the future. I could still feel the warmth of his fingers on my skin. The way he'd looked at me, like he'd wanted to lean in and kiss me right then and there. Shivers danced down my arms at the possibility.

My daydream evaporated when I turned the corner. Sprawled out on the floor at the foot of the stairs was a figure. I hurried closer, and sucked in a sharp breath. Her face was covered by a curtain of bright red hair, but I knew it was her. Celine.

I touched two trembling fingers to her neck, and a wave of dizziness washed over me. A pulse. It was weak, but it was there. Her eyes were closed but they twitched at my touch.

Blood oozed from her forehead, and her lips were split and swollen. Vicious red burns marred her bare arms and hands, and even this close, I could barely see any rise and fall of her chest. I rocked back on my heels, staring down at her.

Whoever had done this hadn't been messing around.

Chapter Fifteen

Word that Celine had ended up in the infirmary spread like wildfire through the whole of the academy. No one had been allowed in to see her, but everyone knew it had to be serious if the healers hadn't been able to get her better in a few days. It had been nearly two weeks since I'd found her and she was still unconscious. The healers had shooed me out of the room the minute I told them I had no idea what had happened. I wasn't useful to them apparently and they said I didn't have a right to know what sort of treatment she needed.

They'd been right about that last part. I had no right to know what they were doing to her. But I had spent the better part of the time she'd been sequestered in the infirmary trying to figure out what could have caused her injuries. I was no expert, but the burns looked similar to what her magic had done to me in Energy Manipulation a few weeks back. Had someone else's magic attacked her own? Except that wouldn't explain why she was still unconscious.

"I'm sure the healers will sort it," Eva offered in the canteen that morning over breakfast.

"They seem stumped," I said around a mouthful of cereal. I'd overheard them yesterday when I'd happened to be passing the medwing, and happened to need to tie my shoelace outside the open door.

"Well, it's not like it's our problem," she said. "It couldn't have happened to a nicer person."

Her words caught my attention. I'd thought the exact same thing months ago when I'd seen one of Celine's lackeys burn herself on the coffee machine not far from where we now sitting.

I tried to put Celine's condition out of my mind. I couldn't afford to be distracted, especially now that we were barely a week from exams. Eva had made me study cards for Botany, and I swear I'd started dreaming of little images of different plants and their properties.

"I got a message from Zachary," I said, hoping to change the subject.

"Has he asked you on a proper date?"

"No." I pouted, then pressed on quickly. "But he said he might be seeing me sooner than we thought."

"That's cryptic."

"Maybe he's trying to surprise me." I rested my chin on my hands and considered the idea. "I mean, he did say he was planning to spend more time with me, and if he wants to start now, I'm not going to be complaining."

"Oh, no, you don't," she said, giving me a stern look that was only partially mock. "If you spend time with him, you're going to forget all about exams and get yourself kicked out."

"Only if I fail everything," I countered.

"Of course. You're right. As long as you pass at least one exam, you'll only get held back a year, which will be so much better."

Yeah, there was that. Okay, so maybe she had a point. Letting Zachary get in my head right now wasn't the smartest move.

The doors directly behind us opened and Instructor Rathbone stepped in. He clapped his hands for attention and utensils clattered down on plates as everyone in the canteen turned their attention to him.

"Dean Bevan requires everyone in the main hall. Please make your way there immediately."

"But I just got my food," Rory called, holding up his plate.

"Sorry," Rathbone said. "It's not optional."

I could hear Rory grumbling under his breath the whole way to the main hall. The atmosphere in the room was thick with tension as low voices whispered, all asking the same question: what was going on? I settled into a seat near the back of the room and Eva scooted in beside me. I spotted Miranda and Jessa down near the front. They had their heads bowed together and I could only imagine they were planning something in Celine's absence. Then again, it had been quiet in class without

Celine there as ringleader—it seemed they were followers rather than leaders, which was probably why she tolerated their presence.

Down at the lectern, Dean Bevan stepped forward. Even from this distance I could see the sweat popping out on his hairline. He was nervous, which didn't bode well for whatever he wanted to share with us.

"Quiet, everyone," he called, his hands held up for silence as his magically amplified voice bounced off the walls.

A hush fell across the room as we all waited for Bevan's announcement. He shifted his weight from one side to the other, like he couldn't quite decide how he wanted to start off.

"I have called you all here to inform you that Braeseth will once again be hosting a team of druid enforcers," he said.

The rumblings in the crowd started low, building to a crescendo until Bevan slammed his palm down on the top of the lectern. Silence fell again and he continued. "As some of you may be aware, a student was attacked recently and remains in stable but critical condition. Our healers have done all they can to aid in the student's recovery, but the Druid Council has generously offered aid from their own healers, as well as a small detachment of security. They will be conducting an investigation into the attack. We take the assault on our students seriously."

"Maybe that's what Zachary meant," Eva whispered in my ear.

The timing matched up. But I didn't like that Bevan was bringing in druids yet again to solve our problems. They'd ended up being the bigger threat to us last semester—or had he forgotten? They acted like we couldn't solve our own problems. We deserved the chance to fix things on our own.

"He's giving in to them too easily," I said.

"They're coming to help Celine," Eva hissed. "I know she's a bitch, but she doesn't deserve to die."

I inclined my head in acknowledgement. Our own healers had got nowhere, and it was clear they weren't going to. Still...

"They're not just sending healers."

"You don't want them to find out what happened?"

"Of course I do. But we could do it ourselves. They say we're supposed to be equal to them, but this proves they're just empty words."

"Quiet, please," Bevan called, raising his hands again until the rabble died down. "I know there may be some... discontent about a renewed druid presence in the academy, but rest assured, the druids are here to render assistance, nothing more, and they have placed themselves under my command for the duration of their stay. They will begin conducting interviews with all students and staff this afternoon on my orders, and I expect you all to cooperate fully with them." He paused and stared around the room, his expression more assertive than I'd ever seen before, underscoring his point.

On cue, the doors beside me opened and three enforcers walked in, including Zachary, kitted out in his full enforcer uniform, complete with black trimmed cloak. He kept his gaze trained forward on Dean Bevan. He might have given me the heads up that he would be coming, but right now he was all business. The way he stood at attention with his hands locked behind his back filled me with unease. At the marketplace, it had been easy to imagine we might be something to each other. But here, I was a misfit, and he was a druid enforcer, and the divide could not have been greater.

"I will not tolerate members of this academy being subject to vicious assaults," Bevan continued. "Whoever was guilty of this attack *will* be found. I suggest you make things easy on yourself by coming forward. Confess your crimes and the council will take that into consideration."

"It's obvious who did it," a third-year guy shouted from the middle of the room. He turned in his seat and pointed a finger right at me. "She did."

I slunk down in my seat as the room full of eyes

turned their attention and judgment on me. I should have seen this coming. It hadn't been bandied about yet, but it also hadn't escaped peoples' notice that I'd been the one to take Celine to the infirmary.

"She totally did this," Jessa shouted from her spot at the front. "She hated poor Celine."

That was an exaggeration. If anything, it was the other way around. But she wasn't wrong that without more to go on, I looked like a reasonable suspect. Shit.

"That's enough," Bevan called, cutting off more people from voicing their reasons for why I must have done it. "The enforcers will conduct a thorough and unbiased investigation and will draw their own conclusions."

This was not what I needed this close to the end of semester. Couldn't I make it a year without something going horribly awry in my world where everyone blamed me something I didn't do? I sunk down even further in my seat and tried to make myself invisible. Of course, my magic decided that exact moment was a brilliant time to actually act on what I wanted. Darkness skittered across my arms and legs. Dammit. Now I really looked like I had something to hide. I willed the shadows to disappear, and as always, they ignored me.

Up front, Dean Bevan cleared his throat. "That is all for now. You are dismissed. Staff will summon you when it is time for your interviews."

It seemed pretty obvious the druids would want to talk to me first, not only because I'd been called out by my fellow students, but because I had been the one to find Celine—and our personal history wasn't exactly helping my case. I tried to prepare myself mentally for what they would ask. As the rest of the students filed out of the room, I tried to recall everything I'd noticed about the surroundings when I'd found Celine.

The floor had been clean except for the blood spilled from her injuries. I hadn't noticed any scorch marks that would indicate the burns touched anything other than her skin. I couldn't fathom why anyone would hate her enough to want to hurt her that badly. Not even me.

"They're gone," Eva said. "We should get going, too."

That was all well and good, but that also assumed I had enough control over my magic to get it to dissipate. I pressed my lips together. I *could* control my magic. I'd done it before, and I was going to do it now.

Slowly, I pulled the magic back into myself, trying to communicate the fact that I didn't need it anymore— something that was easier said than done when my fight or flight response still wanted to protect me from the harassment I knew was waiting for me beyond the doors of the main hall.

The air of the room was cool against my skin as the

shadows finally faded from existence and I suppressed a shiver. I looked around the empty hall, expecting to see at least one person in a position of authority waiting to drag me away to be interrogated, or more likely, the entire trio of enforcers. But it was just me and Eva. Zachary had disappeared with the other enforcers without so much as a word to me. I was more than a little irritated that he hadn't even acknowledged my presence. Even when everyone was jumping on the 'Norah's the worst' bandwagon, he'd kept his attention focused on the front of the room. Like he didn't have any sort of emotional connection with me at all. Next to me, Eva twisted a long lock around her finger. She wouldn't meet my gaze.

"You know I didn't do anything to her, right?" I canted my head, scrutinising her face closely. I needed to know she had my back.

She didn't answer right away. "I want to believe that's true, Nor."

"What's that supposed to mean?" I demanded.

"You did have it out with her before we left, and we did split up when we got back, so..."

Unbelievable. She was *supposed* to be my friend.

"Eva, I didn't do this," I insisted. "She was a mess and unconscious when I found her."

"I'm just trying to think of what they'd say and how they would present it," she said, but I didn't need her magic to know it wasn't the truth. It was a weak attempt to mollify me.

"I don't need you to be playing devil's advocate," I snapped. "I need to know that my best friend has my back."

"I have your back," she said and took my hands in hers. "Always. And if you say you didn't do it…" She sucked in a breath and nodded. "I believe you. But I wouldn't rely on the druids to find the answers. If you want to be sure the right person goes down for the attack, you're going to need to do some digging."

She was right. I didn't want to play detective, but I couldn't afford to leave my fate to chance. I'd cooperate with their investigation, but I wasn't about to assume they'd get the right person in the end. The druids were far from infallible. Last year had taught me that much.

Dragging myself to my feet, I led the way out of the room. I scanned the entry hall, but no one seemed to be looking for me, or waiting to drag me away in chains. Small mercies, I guessed.

I wasn't sure where to start, and the only people likely to know about Celine's movements before the attack were hardly going to share their insights with me. I spotted the door to Bevan's office open, and Miranda stepped inside, followed by one of the enforcers.

The door closed with an echoing thud as they

disappeared from view. In a way, it made sense they would want to talk to Celine's closest friends—or groupies—first. They could establish what she'd been doing when she was attacked. They'd be coming for me soon enough. Miranda would see to that. I was standing there in the middle of the entryway trying to decide my next move when the tiny hairs on the nape of my neck prickled. Someone was watching me, but when I glanced over my shoulder, no-one was looking my way.

"Can we talk?" Zachary's voice came from right beside me and I'm not embarrassed to admit I let out a little squeal as I rounded on him.

"Don't do that," I snapped, reflexively swatting his arm in distress.

"Come with me," he said and nodded up the corridor, not reacting to me slapping him. The look he gave Eva said it was a private conversation.

I swallowed down the lump of fear choking the air from my throat as I trailed him, leaving Eva behind.

The interrogation was about to begin.

Chapter Sixteen

I tried not to panic as he led me into an empty lecture room. It wasn't that I feared he would do horrible things to me, or at least, that's what the logical part of my mind said. But a smaller part whispered that he was a druid enforcer, and I was a suspect, and he wasn't acting like the Zachary who knew me. At all. He looked all business as he sat leaned against the desk at the front of the room. He held out a hand and a pulse of yellow energy emitted from it, pulling the door closed with a bit of his air magic.

"Okay, you're starting to worry me," I said, hoping to break the tension.

"They're going to question you," he said, like I didn't already know that. "But I wanted to talk to you first."

"So… this isn't my interview?" I arched a brow. "This feels like you're breaking the rules for me."

"Not exactly breaking the rules. But I figured if there's anything unflattering I should know, it's better coming from you now so I can help… manage expectations."

It sounded so clinical. "Oh, come on, not you, too? You can't believe I had anything to do with this."

"I know what I've heard about her injuries, and I know that your magic can be unpredictable. Plus, and this definitely is breaking the rules, but at least three people we've already spoken to mentioned you had a very public altercation with her earlier in the day."

"Yes, I got into it with her because she was being a homophobic idiot and because I'm tired of her trying to tell me I don't belong here. But I didn't attack her. If I'd really wanted her to suffer, I'd have just kept walking and left her there."

"One student also mentioned at the start of semester there have been accidents in class. Magic going awry. There've been injuries not unlike what happened to Celine. All when you happen to be around."

"What?"

I sat down in a seat across from where he perched and tried to recall what he was talking about. Then it started to come back to me. The girl who'd been talking shit about me at the very start of last semester. And then there'd been the mishap during the study group. Miranda's accident in the canteen. The girl in the corridor after runes. He was right. I'd been there every time. Shit. It really did look bad, worse than I'd even thought. But I hadn't done a thing. I was innocent.

I tried to keep the panic from my voice and didn't quite pull it off. "I'm not some crazy person out to get back at every person who talks shit about me, I swear."

He smirked. "You'd be at it forever if you did."

Some of the panic eased, and I forced a weak smile. "Thanks for acknowledging my mediocre command of magic. It really brightens a girl's day."

"I'm just speaking the truth," he replied.

"But you do believe me?"

"I know the bravery I saw in you last year when you stepped up to fight to protect people who spent the year hating you for something you couldn't change. That takes courage and heart. That's not the kind of person who lashes out at others."

"Do they really think there's some sort of pattern? Until you said something, I hadn't even remembered those other things. They all seemed minor."

"We have to explore every possibility and that seems to be one we should pursue. Generally, people who commit acts like this don't do it just once. They build up to it. They take aim at others with some sort of connection to the person they really want to hurt."

I nodded. "Do your healers know what's wrong with Celine?"

"They're with her now. I'm sure they'll get her sorted out. The council sent two of our most experienced healers when your dean reached out to them for help."

Wait, *Bevan* had reached out to them? I'd assumed that the druids were shoving their control down our throats again, not trusting us to handle our own affairs.

But they'd come because Bevan asked for help. He must really have been worried about Celine to invite them here. And they'd come to protect the life of one unclassified—a criminal, at that?

Whatever. If they were helping us, it was probably for their own agenda. Trying to prevent an uprising or something. It wouldn't take much to shatter the strained peace between us. If you could call this peace.

"There's something else I wanted to talk to you about," Zachary said, a touch of hesitancy to his voice. My heart fluttered, and I stilled it immediately. It was pretty damned clear from his face he didn't want to talk about *that*. If anything, he looked a little frustrated.

"Oh?"

He raked his fingers through his hair and looked away for a moment. Whatever it was had really touched a nerve. Was this why he'd been more distant during our meetup at the market? Had I unknowingly said or done something that pissed him off?

"Come on," I said. "Out with it."

"You haven't told me about *everything* that happened this year."

"Uh, excuse me?" Was he talking about just now, when we were discussing whether or not I might be a dangerous criminal, or back at the marketplace, on our not-date? Because I could hardly be blamed for not fitting an entire year's worth of events into the time it took to have a coffee. "What are you talking about?"

"I'm talking about you not taking the Enforcer Academy's offer to train there."

I gaped at him. How did he know about that? I hadn't broadcast that the offer had come along, and I'd turned Bevan down ages ago. I hadn't even mentioned it to Kelsey. In fact, I'd barely given it another thought since I'd told Bevan to forget the whole idea. So how the hell did Zachary know about it?

"And I suppose you just happen to know all about that, do you?" It came out more defensive than I'd planned.

"Actually, I do," he replied.

My irritation shifted to disbelief. "How?"

"Christ, Norah, who do you think told them it would be a good idea to give you a shot in the first place?" he snapped.

I blinked at him, dumbfounded. He'd told them I was worth looking at for their little pet project? No, not their pet project. *His* pet project.

"That's stupid, why would you do that?"

My words must have caught him off guard because he stared at me in silence, lips moving as if he were trying to find the words to express himself. Finally, he bent double and I thought I heard soft burbles of laughter coming from his lips. It was only a guess given that I couldn't see his face. His shoulders hooked as the sound increased. Definitely laughter.

"Sorry," he gasped and straightened. His cheeks were rosy and his hair hung in his eyes in a maddeningly attractive way. I wanted to be mad at him, not wishing I could reach over and brush it out of his face. "It's just, you really don't see how good you are. How much potential you have."

"You've seen me in action," I said, rolling my eyes.

"Yes, I have. You could be brilliant at a job like this if you just gave it a chance."

"So, I have good days. But they're few and far between. My magic glitches all the damned time. I'm supposed to know how to control it and I don't. I *can't*."

"That's why you're here, Norah. To learn. It isn't going to click all at once. Hell, it might even not happen until you've graduated. The point is that they're giving you the basics. And I really did put my neck on the line telling the head of the academy to bring you in."

A wave of guilt crashed into me, twisting in my gut. He'd put so much effort into this, and I'd just discarded it out of hand, assuming the worst of the druids. *Like always,* a little voice whispered in my head.

"I'm sorry," I said, and meant it. "But if you really knew me, you wouldn't have bothered wasting your time."

"That's the thing, I do know you. I saw what you went through last year and you came out it the other side stronger than when you went in. You want to give people justice, no matter what their bloodline says."

"It's not that I don't appreciate the compliments, but I just don't see it the way you do. I'm not good enough to be here most days. Why embarrass myself being with a bunch of druids who already think I'm less than them?"

He reached over and took my hands in his. "Because that's the only way we're going to fix things around here. I don't think you're lesser just because you weren't born a druid, Norah. You're brilliant and you've got a bigger heart than anyone gives you credit for. You need to see that."

"You're just saying that because you want me to forgive you for ghosting me."

"I'm serious, Norah. I believe in you, and I think we need to start trusting each other as a whole if the divide between druids and not is ever going to close."

"I'm just one person," I said.

"But you aren't alone."

I pulled free of his grip and paced the short distance between the end of the desk and the door. "So, do you believe that I had nothing to do with what happened to Celine?"

"I do. And I'll turn in my statement from today and my opinion on your innocence, but there's only so much I can do to stop the others from zeroing in on you."

I heard the implied statement behind his words. I had to give him someone else to focus on as a suspect. Because despite everything he'd said, my kind didn't trust his, and they were never going to open up to him willingly. Of course, I was hardly in a much better position. Half the academy didn't like me, and even the ones who gave me encouraging looks from across the canteen were probably terrified of me now. Maybe I could convince Eva to use her lie detecting power on everyone. It would certainly save me some time.

"I know what you're thinking," Zachary said after a moment silence passed between us.

"Those air powers suddenly give you telepathy?" I snorted.

"You don't think you can handle this, but you can. Besides, you've got as much motivation as the real assailant to sort it out."

He wasn't wrong. "I suppose that's all the ringing endorsement I need to begin my career as a snoop."

"I could think of worse professions. Especially if it means getting to spend more time with you."

He leaned toward me, and I'd have to be blind not to see that he was trying to not so subtly make a move on me. I stepped closer and took his hands in mine. "As much as I'd really like to give you a proper kiss right now, with my luck, the whole bloody academy would come marching through that door to interrupt. And neither of us needs the heat of you playing favourites."

He let out a heavy sigh and pulled his hands from mine. "You're right. Of course you are. I should know better. I came here to do a job, not fall…" He cut himself off and my heart skipped a beat as my brain imagined four very specific words completing that sentence.

Before I could say anything else, his head whipped to the door and he stood up straighter.

"You should get back to the interrogating," I murmured. And I needed to make a plan for how I was going to hunt down the real culprit.

He gave me a smile and made for the door.

"Just remember you aren't alone in this, Norah."

Chapter Seventeen

To my surprise, it took Zachary and his enforcer buddies a full week to bring me into be questioned. I made my way into Bevan's office and Zachary wouldn't meet my eye. The tension in the air was palpable as I perched on the edge of the chair closest to the door. I couldn't help being reminded of the time he'd been in here with me when I'd learned about Micah's fate.

"Norah Sheehan," the other male enforcer said, settling into a chair across from me.

"Last I checked," I answered. I couldn't help being snarky. I'd been waiting for this little chat for days and I'd been on edge the whole time. And just like I assumed they were nowhere closer to finding the real person behind Celine's attack, neither was I.

"I am Enforcer Dominic Loughty. I'm sure you're not unaware that it's common knowledge amongst the other students that there was a certain... tension between you and the victim," he began.

"She doesn't like me and I'd be lying if I said the feeling wasn't mutual," I said, because it wasn't like there was any point in trying to hide it. "But I'd never want to hurt her."

I watched Zachary from the corner of my eye. He

stood silently behind his colleague. Either he hadn't told them that we had history, or they credited his professionalism that he wouldn't let it get in the way of him doing his job.

"Even though we have records from staff indicating you have been sent to the infirmary for injuries inflicted by the victim?" Dominic said.

I stared in surprise at his words, and my eyes snapped back to him. I should have realised they would have talked to the instructors. Rathbone and Glover might not have wanted to sell me out, but they'd have been obligated to tell the enforcers everything that had happened between us—including Celine's attacks on me. Which gave me a pretty strong motive to lash back out at her.

"Okay, yes, we had issues, and yes, she kicked my arse a few times. And yeah, that pissed me off because I put that exact same arse on the line to stop her spending more than a few weeks in jail last year."

"That doesn't sound like much of a denial of a motive," the enforcer noted. I could see from his hardened expression that he'd already made up his mind that I was the one behind it all.

"Er, did you not just hear me say that I saved her from rotting last year?" Zachary winced and gave me a small shake of his head behind the other enforcer, and I sucked in a quick breath and pressed on. "Look, if you talked to anyone in this place, you'll know that my magic is rubbish. I can barely make it work most of the time. I saw what happened to Celine—when I got help for her, by the way. Those injuries were awful, but they were targeted and precise. I do not have, and have never had, that level of control."

The enforcer turned to look at Zachary. "You've seen her magic in action. Does that seem credible to you?"

"I will admit that I have not seen her control her magic with consistent precision."

Not the worst answer he could have given. A part of me had been expecting him to also add that he was my alibi, but that might be pushing things too far. But he wasn't the only one who'd known I was off grounds.

"I wasn't even on grounds when she got attacked. I was at Fantail market with my dorm mate. We were gone a couple of hours."

The other enforcer narrowed his gaze. "Can anyone besides your dorm mate confirm that?"

Indecision flickered across Zachary's face. I'd just put him in a horrible spot, which was exactly what I'd been trying to avoid. I wanted to give him some sort of signal that it was okay to keep quiet—I knew he wouldn't lie, but he didn't have to tell the truth, either—but Dominic was watching me too closely.

Zachary lifted his chin. "I can."

That was enough to make his fellow enforcer actually spin the chair a quarter turn. "What?"

"I was at the market, too. We ran into each other. We became acquainted last year while I was stationed here. We spoke for a while at Fantail before she left. Based on the healers' report, it seems unlikely she'd have had time to return and carry out the attack."

The enforcer stood and stalked out of the room. Zachary stepped past the desk to follow, and I tried to mouth 'I'm sorry' but he wouldn't look at me. The door still sat ajar, and I tried not to look too interested in the tongue-lashing Zachary was presently receiving.

Bevan watched from off to one side and I could read the worry on his face. The lines creasing his forehead were the obvious sign but the way his shoulders slumped told me he had bigger concerns than an enforcer being overly friendly with one of his students.

"You don't really think I'd go after her, do you?" I said softly.

"Someone in this academy did," he said.

"And everyone assumes it was me because Celine decided I was the bane of her existence." I narrowed my eyes. "But that's not what you're really worried about, is it?"

His brow crinkled further. "I don't know what you're

talking about."

"It's obvious," I said flatly. "Under your leadership, Micah and the others were able to shut down Braeseth and three of the druid academies. Since then, we've nearly had a coup, and we've had druids trying to strip us of our magic. And now you've got someone attacking students and the druids have to swoop in and save the day again. If you're trying to prove that we're able to govern ourselves and handle our own stuff, you aren't exactly convincing anyone of that."

His jaw hung slack as he looked at me. My words crackled between us in the silence and a tiny part of me felt bad for dumping all of that on him. That part whispered that he knew his faults and that this situation looked bad to the outside world. As much as he claimed we were equal to the druids, we weren't. Not really. And maybe, in some twisted way, that was what Micah had been trying to prove.

Before Bevan could speak, the doors burst open and Zachary reappeared, followed not only by Dominic, but one of the healers, too. I hadn't seen them leave the infirmary since they'd arrived. Not even for meals.

The healer looked at Bevan and said, "She's awake."

The tension in the room suddenly burst like a soap bubble and Bevan exhaled loudly. "Oh, thank goodness."

"She's not talking yet, but she can at least follow

simple instructions," the healer continued as if I wasn't there.

Dominic looked at me and said, "You can go. But don't think we're finished."

I battled the temptation to flip him off and tell him to just go talk to Celine. She'd be able to clear all of this up. And no matter how much she probably wanted to tell them it was me, I didn't think even she would stoop to that level.

I retreated to the dorm, desperate to find Eva and debrief, but our room was empty. I stood in the doorway for a moment, wondering where she could have gone. And then remembered exams were right around the corner. She usually studied in the library, and she usually forgot that she had human needs—like eating and drinking. I stopped by the canteen to grab some coffee and fruit on the way, and hoped I wouldn't incur the librarian's wrath for trying to sneak the contraband in around her precious books.

In the end, sneaking it into the library was easier than it should have been because the librarian who usually sat sentry by the front of the space was missing. I tried not to let that bother me as I wound my way through to Eva's favourite spot by the back of the library.

"There you are," I said when she finally came into view.

She started at my words and sat up, trying to shuffle whatever she was reading out of view. "Don't sneak up on a girl, Nor."

"We're in a library. I think that's sort of the default mode of transit. Anyway, since when do you freak out when I walk in?" I set the coffee and food in front of her and mimed eating and drinking.

Her cheeks darkened in embarrassment, and she snatched up the coffee first, gulping it down greedily.

"How'd your interview go?" Her words came from around the rim of the cup.

My curiosity about what she didn't want me to see warred with my desire to spill everything from my brief but nerve-wracking interview with the enforcers. My curiosity lost the battle and I said, "They still think I did it. And I'm pretty sure even though some people were trying to have my back, they kind of painted a target on it. But Zachary alibied me and that got his enforcer buddy all mad."

"What happened?" She leaned forward, elbows propped on the edge of the table, cup clasped between both hands.

"They left and I couldn't really hear what they were saying. That's not even the biggest thing. Celine is awake."

Eva's eyes went wide. "So they can actually clear it all

up, then."

"I hope so. Because I am tired of everyone thinking I'm some sort of monster. I didn't start this rivalry with her. It's all in her head."

Eva nodded and took a bite from an apple. "So, how do you feel about Zachary standing up to defend you?"

"It wasn't as much a defence as I left him no choice. He told me to be honest and so I told him you and I were at the market when the attack happened."

"And he chimed in that you were on a date?" She smirked.

"No. And it wasn't a date." This whole thing with Celine made me doubt we would ever actually have a proper date. I'd put him in a painful spot with his people, even if it hadn't been on purpose, and I wouldn't blame him if he never wanted to speak to me again.

"Do you have any idea who might have done it?"

I shook my head. "I've been trying to figure it out all week. And I keep coming to the same conclusion as everyone else. I'm the best suspect."

"But, as you said, we both know you have an alibi."

A chair nearby creaked and I turned to find a familiar face staring back at me. The first-year girl who'd ambushed me at the start of last semester in the canteen. What was her name? Bethany? Brenda? Dammit, why was I so terrible with names?

"Sorry, I didn't mean to eavesdrop," she said, convincing precisely no-one.

"Been a while…" I trailed off, hoping she'd fill in her name so I didn't look like a total bitch.

"Belinda," she offered helpfully. "I just thought you should know that not everyone thinks you did it. Though, between us, I wouldn't have blamed you if you had done it. But I think the druids are more interested in that it looked like someone escalated the attacks."

"Escalated?" I repeated. "What else have you heard?"

"Well, apparently the infirmary has to report injuries to the dean," Belinda said, scooting her chair closer. "At least when they seem to be unexplained. I heard there were at least three other students who had injuries. Minor compared to Celine, but still kind of similar."

"There was that girl on the first day of Energy Manipulation," Eva said.

"And Rory did get blasted during that study session," I added. But I already knew about those.

I tried to think back to who all was present when those things happened. There'd been a whole room full of people both times. And no one stood out. I needed to see that log in the infirmary and find out if there were any other attacks we didn't know about. Maybe I could compile a list of everyone who'd been at both scenes—though so far that seemed to be most of our year.

Several not-so-hushed whispers drew my attention and I turned to see Miranda and Jessa glaring at me from a distance.

They both raised their hands to show me they had energy crackling along their palms. They were ready for a fight. But unlike their leader, they didn't initiate. Maybe they were too afraid to take me on, if they really believed I'd put Celina in a coma for weeks. But then, another thought started to take root in my mind.

Celine and her goons had been in all the places where other people had been hurt and I knew that she was capable of messing with other people's magic. I was living proof, and just the thought of it made my hands and back ache with the reminder of what that magic felt like. And Celine was definitely angry enough that I was still around that she might fake her own attack. I wouldn't doubt that she was more skilled than Miranda and Jessa. So maybe they'd only intended to injure her a little, and the magic had gotten away from them. Maybe she'd planned to have them point the finger at me and somehow get me kicked out as revenge for getting them sent to prison. It made sense.

"What?" I finally said, addressing the girls shooting daggers my way.

They looked at each other but didn't speak. I guess they hadn't heard the news that Celine was awake yet. No doubt they'd know soon enough. Nothing stayed secret in this academy for long.

Maybe I should help them along. "You know your ringleader woke up. Or so I hear from the druid healers, anyway."

Miranda's lips turned upward in a smile, and she dragged Jessa away, leaving me, Belinda, and Eva there at the table. I turned back to them. "What if Celine did this to herself to try and get back at me?"

"You really think you'd put herself in harm's way like that? I mean, she's power hungry, sure, but she's not stupid," Eva said.

"I think it sounds possible," Belinda said. "Especially if you were both around when the other accidents happened."

I'd have to pass it along to Zachary—I didn't think Dominic would be particularly receptive to anything I had to say in my own defence—but I'd give them chance to interview Celine and for the healers to make sure she was actually healed of her injuries first. Until they released her from the infirmary, I planned to stay as far from her as humanly possible. And after, preferably.

Belinda stared at me for a moment longer and then seemed to recognise she was an awkward third wheel. She gave a small wave and scooted her chair back to her own table.

A moment of silence passed between me and Eva and then that curiosity about what she was hiding rose to the surface again. "So, what were you looking at when I came in? You seemed awfully keen that I didn't see it."

"It's nothing," she said.

"Come on, spill it, Eva. You know I'm not going to blab to anyone."

"Mum's got me trying to find my dad in old yearbooks," she finally admitted. She moved some of the papers she'd spread across the table to reveal several years of student rosters. "She said she may not have magic, but she thinks it's important for me to know where mine comes from."

"I thought you gave up the search after your manifestation event?"

"I did. But, I don't know, it feels like it might be important now. The world is changing out there. Tensions between unclassifieds and druids is high. We can all feel it. And maybe knowing who my father is will give me some sense of where I really belong."

I gestured around us and grinned. "You belong here. You're kicking arse."

"I still feel like there's more to the story that Mum doesn't know. But so far, I haven't found anything. There's too many people, and Mum thinks he even gave her a fake name."

"If you do find him, what are you going to say to him?" I probed. I was pretty sure from what she'd told me before she wanted to chew him out for knocking up her mum and then ghosting on the pair of them, but this seemed like a great length to go to just to yell at a guy.

"I don't know. I know I was mad at him for a while, but I think I'd just like to know who he is and if he knew about me."

It wasn't unreasonable. And I of everyone knew that family was complicated, especially when it came to us unclassifieds. We didn't fit anywhere, not really, and that was the whole problem, wasn't it?

"Well, I'm sure you'll sort it out. And in the meantime, you promised you would make sure I don't fail botany again."

She chuckled and pulled out her botany textbook. In here, we could pretend to just be two second years trying not to fail our exams. For a little while, at least.

Chapter Eighteen

Celine had finally returned to the dorms two days ago, and the druid healers had left as soon as she'd settled back into her room. Apparently, their work here was finished. No one really knew what they'd done to get Celine awake and moving again. Even our own healers were being tight-lipped about it, aside from praising the skill and talents of the druid healers. If the circle's motive in sending them here was to repair bridges, I had to grudgingly admit that it had been well played—they'd come out of it looking like benign saviours, despite the fact that two of the enforcers would be staying on to continue their investigations.

My own intercommunity relations were not going so smoothly—Zachary had been keeping his distance since my interview. It hurt a little, but I didn't really blame him. I was surprised his superiors hadn't decided to haul him off for having a conflict of interest in the situation, but maybe they were giving his professionalism a little more credit than that. Maybe he'd just told them there was nothing going on between us, which certainly seemed to be true right now.

Celine had avoided everyone except her two sycophants since leaving the medwing, and I did my best not to get in her line of sight. I didn't need her lashing out. Not when exams were only a day off. Even though she'd been released from the infirmary, she still hadn't made an appearance in class. If she wasn't up to taking her exams in a couple of days, she was going to have to resit the entire year. Not that I'd have any objection to not having to see her every day, but still... it seemed a little harsh.

I hadn't had too much time to dwell on it, because with exams looming, our instructors had been pressuring us to spend every spare moment practicing and revising. Energy Manipulation remained one of my worst subjects. We'd been working on energy shields the last few weeks but I still hadn't managed to manifest one fully yet. Secretly, I was hoping for a miracle akin to last year's exam, because that seemed like my best—and only—chance of scraping a pass.

Rathbone cleared his throat, and when my gaze snapped back to him, he inclined his head and raised a brow at me. Okay, so maybe he had a point: my chances of passing his class might dramatically increase if I actually stayed focus for an entire lesson. We'd been here all of five minutes and already my attention was drifting. But that was hardly my fault, what with the whole lack of sleep thing I had going on right now.

"As I was saying," he continued, "We'll be continuing

our work on shield projection today in preparation for your exams. Up to this point, they've been still connected to you physically, but today, that's going to change."

"Are you telling us what's on the exam?" Rory called from the back of the room.

Rathbone gave us a wry smile and a shrug. "Your exam will be entirely practical in nature. I don't see that it hurts for you to know which skills to hone. I'd prefer not to see every one of my students fail. It looks bad on my record."

There were a couple of chuckles, and then Reggie spoke up.

"Will it be like last year, with the barriers so we can't see each other?" he asked.

"Well, I can't have anyone cheating now, can I?" Rathbone answered.

The fear that had begun burning in my chest subsided slightly. At least no one but Rathbone would be able to see me if I floundered. Or if my shield manifested as pure shadow like it had at least half the times I'd tried this particular exercise. The fact he expected me to manifest the thing and disconnect it from my body made my stomach churn. I'd never seen anyone use magic like that and I'd never attempted it. I was nowhere near that standard yet, and if that was what it took to pass his exam, I was totally screwed.

The door creaked, and every head in the room snapped round to watch as it swung open.

Celine paused in the doorway, looking in. She was paler than last time I'd seen her and her expression was haunted, with none of the usual haughtiness she usually wore. She looked hesitant, clutching her books to her like a shield, and a very small part of me almost felt glad she'd been taken down a peg, but even I wasn't enough of a monster to revel in her obvious distress. I knew she'd been subjected to serious injuries and even if she was awake and moving about, that didn't mean she'd fully healed. She wasn't the only one who wasn't over it completely. I hadn't told anyone, not even Eva, but I'd been having dreams about the druids who'd tried to steal our magic except this time, they were somehow the ones responsible for attacking Celine, which I knew didn't make a lick of sense, but that didn't get me any closer to getting a solid night's sleep.

"Ah, Celine," Rathbone said loudly, cutting across the whispers that were racing round the room. "Dean Bevan informed me you would be joining us again. Please, take a seat."

"Yes, Instructor Rathbone," she said, and stepped into the room, shutting the door behind her. She tried to look smug as she crossed the room to join Jessa and Miranda but the skin around her eyes and lips was pinched, and her stride just a little too hurried to be relaxed. She was nervous being around people again. I also think for the first time in her life, she might have been uncomfortable in the spotlight. Even if it was just to acknowledge she was once more gracing us with her presence.

For my part, I dragged my eyes away from her and kept them forward. The last thing I needed was anyone thinking I was staring daggers at her, or plotting some sort of revenge. The enforcers were no closer to solving her attack than I was, and things were starting to get tense, especially for those of us who were here last year. Plenty of people would be happy to see them go, even if it meant dragging an innocent and somewhat incompetent witch with them. Shockingly, I didn't share the sentiment. At least, not that part.

"As I was saying," Rathbone said, and the class resettled their attention on him, "You will be disconnecting from your shields today. Now, before anyone panics, casting a shield that isn't attached to you isn't that complicated. It's still an extension of your magic, you just want it to have the ability to move beyond you. Watch."

He held up one hand and a perfect sphere of energy manifested in his palm. I caught his gaze narrow ever so slightly before he tossed the energy ball into the air and caught it with his other hand. He elongated it into a shield between his fingertips and then tilted it at an angle, gripping it in one hand. With his other, he gestured for the students in my row to duck. I obliged but was still able to see it go whizzing above our heads and collide with the wall. The runes protecting the classroom lapped up the energy, dissipating it in seconds.

"It's not a physical thing as much as a mental one," he explained.

Great, just what I needed. More mental skills. But I'd have to give it a go. Rathbone was one of the few instructors who actually liked me and I hated to disappoint him. So, as everyone turned their focus to their own hands, I sat there and did my best to conjure up a shield devoid of shadows.

I could feel my magic deep inside, like it was hibernating. It was there, but it didn't want to come out and play. Which made me want to scream. Was a little electrical current too much to ask for? I could hear the snap and crackle of my classmates having success at the very least generating energy balls.

I did my best to block out the sound and concentrate. I closed my eyes—which wouldn't have been the best move if I were in a life-or-death scenario but this was class so it was only somewhat life threatening—and tried to picture the energy ball forming in my hands, all glossy and rippling with blue and purple sparks. *Come on, just give me something.* My heart hammered in my chest as I felt something stir within me. My lips started to turn up in a smile when I realised it wasn't just electrical current rising to meet my desire. It was tinged in *shadow.*

Dammit. I tried to fight against them and push them away. I didn't need them fouling up the spell I was trying to cast. But as soon as the shadows touched my intention, the shadowy bubble of energy materialised between my fingers. I felt the sleekness against my fingertips, almost like liquid undulating over my skin. I opened my eyes to see it sitting there on the desk. Tiny tendrils of shadow coiled around my hands still connecting it to me. I was never going to pass this dumb exam if I couldn't even access the right type of magic.

I was still trying to work out how to do that when a loud shriek shattered my focus. I twisted round to find Celine's mouth hanging open in horror. Her hands shook and her body bobbed back and forth.

"It's gone!" she shouted, eyes wild.

Rathbone was off his perch on the front of his desk and looming over Celine's desk in an instant.

"What's gone?" he asked.

She tilted her head up, turned, and looked right at me. I caught the unshed tears in her eyes and the terror on her face. She turned back to Rathbone, blinked rapidly, and her voice came out as a whisper so quiet that I almost didn't catch it.

"My magic. I can't call it up anymore."

"Let's take a breath and not panic," he said.

"It's her fault," she added, jabbing a finger in my direction.

Murmurs flew around the classroom, wondering if it was true and what had I done to make her magic vanish. The calm demeanour faltered on Rathbone's face as the murmurs grew louder.

"You did this!" Celine shouted at me. "What have you done to my magic?"

"I didn't do anything," I protested.

"Of course you did," she snarled. "Who else would have done this to me? I'm going to make you pay for this!"

She was out of her seat before I could blink, barrelling towards me. I was on my feet without even meaning to stand and shadow sprang from my hands to coil protectively around me. I did nothing to stop it. She'd put me in the medwing more than once, and I wasn't about to let it happen again.

Rathbone moved quickly, stepping between us.

"Enough." His voice was firm, and Celine faltered, settling for staring daggers at me over his shoulder. He turned to me, his expression hard. "Lose the magic.

Now."

I swallowed hard and nodded, forcing the magic from my body and into the ground, where the runes blazed as they absorbed and neutralised it.

Rathbone turned to address the rest of the class.

"Everyone, revision is over. You know what you need to practise for my exam. So, go do it." He pointed to me and Celine. "You two, stay."

I cast Eva a worried look but she gave me a discreet thumbs up and mouthed 'You'll be fine'. I wished I had her confidence, because there was no way in this world conjuring magic like that had done a thing to help dissuade anyone of my guilt. I was such an idiot. And I was so beyond screwed.

"Sit, both of you," Rathbone commanded as the last student slipped out of the room, shutting the door behind them. I sank back into my seat, and Celine stalked a few paces away before reluctantly dropping into one.

"Now, explain what you mean by you think your magic is gone," Rathbone said, looking straight at Celine.

"I can't feel it. It was there before and now... it's like it's just gone."

"You were looked over by the druid healers. Did they tell you there was cause for concern about your magic?"

She chewed her lower lip and finally shook her head. "No. They said I was fine." She turned to me again. "But she did something to me that they can't see."

I snorted and arched a brow at her. "Oh, come on, you don't believe that for a second. We both know I'm shite at magic. There's no way I could do something to you that the druids couldn't spot a mile off."

I wanted to add that she assumed I cared more about her than I actually did but I held my tongue. I was looking bad enough as it was, and I didn't need to be the one adding fuel to the fire.

"I know you did something. You were jealous of how good my magic is so you took it away, so I'd be as pathetic as you."

"Even if I could do that, which again, I think we all know I can't, why would I bother? You might find this hard to believe, but my world doesn't revolve around you." So much for holding my tongue.

"Enough!" Rathbone's voice boomed in the confines of the classroom and I jumped. He pointed a figure at Celine. "I'm assuming you spoke with the enforcers conducting the investigation into your attack."

She had the nerve to roll her eyes at him. They were mysteriously devoid of tears now. "Obviously."

"And you told them everything you remembered about the incident."

"Du… yes."

"Did you actually see Norah attack you?"

Finally, someone asking the important questions.

"Well… no."

I beamed in spite of myself. She'd just vindicated me, whether she wanted to admit it or not.

"It's all a little fuzzy still. I was in the corridor and then there was just… pain. From behind."

Bugger. That didn't help at all.

"But I remember seeing someone's face standing over me before I blacked out. They had dark hair."

I snorted again, and Rathbone twisted round to glare in my direction.

That described half the student population—not to mention a big segment of the general population—and we all knew it.

"Do you think maybe it's a case of nerves? A bit of post-traumatic stress?" Rathbone suggested.

"What do you mean?" Celine murmured.

"I'm guessing you haven't tried using your magic for anything big since the attack." He paused long enough for her to nod. "And I think we can all agree what happened to you was traumatic. It stands to reason that there would be some residual fear associated with your magic. Give it some time."

"But what am I supposed to do about exams? I can't not take them. They'll kick me out."

"I'm sure Dean Bevan will understand and make

some allowances," Rathbone answered.

Celine pouted but said nothing more, settling instead for glaring sullenly in my direction.

"Now, Celine, do everyone a favour and stop blaming Norah for what happened. Not when you have no evidence to back up your claim."

I had to admit I was feeling pretty good about the situation now. She couldn't say that she never said she didn't see me do it, not when there was an instructor ready and willing to back me up.

He rounded on me, his expression terse. "That goes for you, too, Norah. There's no need to be bickering with each other. Just stay out of each other's way. Sit your exams and go home for summer. Do I make myself clear?"

I nodded in silence. The intensity of his gaze made my heart jump into my throat. Sometimes I forgot how skilled a magic wielder he was, even if he was mild mannered most of the time. Throwing those energy shields around earlier was a stark reminder of the damage he could do if someone crossed him.

"I said, do I make myself clear?" he repeated, looking from me to Celine and back again.

"Yes, Instructor," we both answered.

"Now, get out of here," he said, and pointed to the door. I almost expected a ripple of energy to emanate from his hand to push it open. Or maybe a gust of air from an unseen druid to tug it loose. Neither happened, and I had to settle for gathering my bag and starting for the door.

Loathe though I was to admit it, Rathbone was right. I needed to put this behind me and focus on getting through exams. I didn't need the drama looming over me. And yet, I still was no closer to figuring out who really attacked Celine, and I couldn't trust it to the druids to clear my name. At least I had more information to go on than before. I knew that they had dark hair. I doubted any of the first years would have been angry enough at Celine to go after her. And they likely didn't have the skills it took to pull off that sort of damage. That meant a second or third year. And my guess was it was someone in our year. For one thing, if the druids were right and someone had been building up to the attack, all the other victims were in our year.

I started to picture everyone in our year with dark hair but didn't get far before Celine stalked up behind me and stepped into the doorway, barring my exit. Our gazes met and I tried to step around her, but she moved with me. I could feel Rathbone's gaze on us as Celine stuck out her hand for me to shake.

"No hard feelings," she said loud enough for Rathbone to hear.

I didn't trust her, but if she was offering peace, even if it was just long enough for both of us to survive exams, I'd take it. So I extended my hand to shake hers and said, "Yeah, no hard feelings."

She looked past me, to Rathbone I assumed, and held my hand in a vice grip until I heard him clear his throat and start moving around his desk. She finally let go and I grit my teeth, my hand throbbing from the pressure. Celine stepped out of the doorway, allowing me into the corridor.

"This isn't over," she hissed in my ear. "You'd better watch your back."

Chapter Nineteen

Celine's words followed me down the corridor and out onto the grounds. I had no idea where Eva had gone but honestly, I wasn't in the mood to have her tell me to not let Celine get to me, anyway. I'd spent months trying not to let her get to me and where had I ended up? With everyone thinking I'd tried to do her in, and even more bloody druid scrutiny. I was so tired of all the looks and judgment. I almost wished I could be back in Micah's shadow where no one noticed me. All of this was just too much for me to handle.

The grounds were deserted. Everyone was probably off studying for exams. Like I should be, except my mind wouldn't settle down. It just kept playing that lesson over and over, proving to me that I had no control over my magic whatsoever. What kind of witch couldn't even conjure a stupid energy ball? They might call this place the Misfit academy, but I was the only misfit around here. Was it really too much to ask to fit in, just once in my life?

I wound my way along the outer wall that enclosed the courtyard area. The gates were somewhere up ahead, and a wardline encircled the whole thing, protecting us from the attention of mundanes—though apparently not druids.

I heaved a sigh as I kept walking, trailing the fingers of one hand along the wall. It wasn't like I could deny that the druids had actually helped us this time, which'd be great, if I didn't get the sense that at least one of them was trying to pin the whole thing on me.

"Thinking about climbing it?"

I jumped and spun around to find Zachary watching me with an amused smile playing across his lips. There were stress lines around his eyes and mouth. I guess he was just as worried as everyone else that they hadn't been able to solve the mystery of Celine's attack yet. Of course, he—I hoped—had the added stress of trying to prove it wasn't me into the bargain.

"Have you come to arrest me?" I asked, a matching smile playing over my lips as I thrust my hands out in front of me, wrists together.

He bent his head towards me conspiratorially. "Maybe we should make a break for it."

"Yeah? Where would we go?"

"Could always open that café we talked about," he said with a smile.

"Sure. If you weren't a druid enforcer and I wasn't a failing misfit."

I started strolling again, and he fell into step beside me.

"Classes aren't going so well, huh?"

I snorted softly. "What gave it away?" I sighed and shook my head. "You know, I think my control might actually be getting worse. Today in Energy Manipulation we were supposed to be manifesting energy shields and detaching them from ourselves. That's the standard everyone else is at. Meanwhile, I can't even conjure an energy ball without my shadows tainting it. Most of the time I can barely access my magic. And then when I am able to, it just doesn't work how I want."

"You'll get it," he said with a shrug. "You just need to stop fighting it."

My feet rooted to the ground, and I glared at him. "I'm not fighting it."

He raised a brow. "Aren't you?"

"Of course not. You think I want my magic to keep crapping out on me?"

"I think you're scared it'll make you like your brother. But it won't, you know."

I shivered and wrapped my arms around myself. My voice came out small.

"What makes you so sure?"

He shook his head with a smile. "You really don't see yourself at all, do you?"

"I see shadows," I said, rolling my eyes. "Lots of shadows. Every damned time I try to conjure an energy ball.”

“And what's so bad about that? Shadows are your unique magic. They're who you are, in the same way my air magic comes from who I am.”

“But the shadows can be dangerous. When they first manifested… you saw what happened.”

“And you've got it under control since then.”

“Not always. Sometimes I can feel it wanting to lash out at people.”

“Magic doesn't have a mind of its own, Norah. It all comes from you. Your emotions, your thoughts. So if you think it wants to lash out at people, that's you.”

“Well then I'm terrified I'm going to hurt someone.” As soon as the words came out of my mouth, I realised I was lucky I hadn't said them while his enforcer buddy in earshot. It would have made me look even guiltier than I already did.

“Why do you think you'll hurt people?” Zachary probed gently.

“Isn't that kind of obvious?”

“Last I checked, your name wasn't Micah, and you weren't locked up in prison,” he answered.

“But I'm related to him, and that darkness had to come from somewhere. His powers let him hurt others and sometimes… sometimes I feel like my magic wants to do that, too.” I didn't add that I sometimes wondered if something in our upbringing had pushed Micah on the path he'd gone down. We'd had the same childhood. So why would I be lucky enough to come out of it any different to him?

"It doesn't mean you are automatically going to turn out evil. I've seen the way you operate, Norah. In the face of adversity, and when those you care about are threatened, you fight for what's right. You need to see that you aren't your brother. Stop fighting your magic. You *can* control it."

"Everyone keeps saying things like that, but I don't know how. I can barely keep up with lessons and I'm so far behind everyone else in my year. Exams are tomorrow and part of me thinks if I just fail everything, they'll expel me and bind my magic and I won't have to worry about all of this."

He pushed off the wall and cupped my chin in his hand, tilting my face to look up at him. It felt like a very sensual gesture, and I hoped he was going to kiss me just to shut me up. For a split second, I pictured it happening, soft and gentle. Then things got a little more adult-rated. Not that I minded one bit.

"You are not going to fail your exams. You are going to pass, and you are going to graduate next year and go on to do something amazing with your life. You are your own worst enemy, Norah. Let the people who believe in you build you up. You hear me?"

I swallowed, my legs suddenly turning to jelly. "Okay."

We stood like that with the tension building between us like until it was something palpable. His lips parted like he wanted to say something else but stopped short. For my part, I had no idea what else to say. Asking him to make a move seemed too bold. Even for the girl who'd kissed him on Valentine's Day.

He finally dropped his hand and turned his attention to a point across the courtyard. His eyes narrowed and I tried to see what he was looking at, but there was nothing out of the ordinary. Not until a yellow blur came rushing toward us. My body tensed as it approached but Zachary didn't look afraid. In fact, he held out a hand and the blur formed into the general shape of a large cat. A lynx, maybe. It wound itself around his legs—definitely a cat—and I thought I heard it purr. Or at least something akin to a breeze rustling leaves.

"Uh, want to fill a girl in on your weird little love fest?" I said.

Zachary didn't address me right away. He reached down towards the translucent creature and pulsed yellow energy from his hand, tracing the shape of the lynx's head and neck from a quarter inch above.

"Sorry, I forgot you two hadn't met. This is my

familiar."

I'd heard the term before, but never seen one. And I had always assumed it was an actual living creature. Not… whatever this thing was.

"Oh, uh, cool. Don't think I saw it when you were here last year."

"They usually stay with us all the time but last year, because of everything that was going on, we were instructed to leave them behind. We couldn't be sure that they wouldn't be used against us. This time, I brought him along. Enforcers bond with their familiars early at the academy. You can't qualify without one."

"So do they, like, help you do magic?"

"Not exactly. When a familiar chooses to bond with us, they act as our guides and guardians."

"Just another perk of being a druid, I suppose."

"One of the best things about being an enforcer," he agreed.

"So do they go where you do, or can they roam free?" I didn't recall seeing any ghostly cats prowling around the café at Fantail Market.

"They are connected to us, but they don't have to be where we are. They're partners, not servants. He's been patrolling the grounds."

The familiar looked up at me and that eerie sense of being watched crept up my spine. Had Zachary been keeping an eye on me the whole time? And if he had been spying on me through his familiar, did that mean he didn't trust me?

The creature leaned over and sniffed at my hand. It felt like a light breeze, tickling the pads of my fingers. I half-expected to be bitten, but instead it opened its mouth in a silent purr. At least it—he—seemed to approve of me.

"He likes you," Zachary said, one corner of his mouth lifting in a smile. "Not that I'm surprised."

The familiar turned back to Zachary and his lips pulled back in a silent growl, then he toward the front of the academy and back to Zachary, pressing his ears to his head.

Zachary's brow knitted together and after a moment, he asked, "Are you sure?"

The familiar opened his mouth again, and again, no sound came out—at least, not one that I could hear. Zachary seemed to have no problem understanding what the creature was trying to convey, though how he could do that was a question for another day. It was fascinating all the same to watch him converse with the creature. Maybe they had a Familiar 101 course at the enforcer academy. The image that popped into my head made me snicker.

"When and where did you see him last?" Zachary's

voice pulled me out of the vision of him chasing around a disobedient cat, trying to tame it.

Another silent yowl issued from the familiar's mouth and Zachary let out an audible exhale. "Well, this isn't great."

"For those of us who don't speak ghost cat, care to translate?"

He rubbed at the back of his neck in a sheepish gesture. It was adorable. "Dominic, the other enforcer who stayed on after the healers left, he's missing."

"What do you mean, missing?"

"He hasn't been seen since this morning. He was near the canteen. Admittedly, he likes his food. So it's possible he loaded up and just went off grounds. But if he doesn't come back, I'm going to have to report it to the Circle. And that is not going to help our cause."

No, it certainly was not. Because if word got back that there was even the slightest chance that something had happened to a druid enforcer while he was in *our* academy, enforcers would be pouring in here by the dozen.

And whatever tentative truce had sprung up between the druids and us would be torn down.

Chapter Twenty

"**What can I** do to help?" I asked at once, fighting to keep the quiver from my voice. "I mean, do you think he has actually gone missing or just gone off for a bit of alone time?"

Zachary shook his head. "I'm not sure. But if we can track him down, then there'll be no reason to report anything out of the ordinary. I can hold off until tomorrow evening, but after that I'm going to have to check in and let my superiors know."

"Do you think whoever attacked Celine might have done something to him?"

"It's possible. But, in all honesty, we're no closer to figuring out who that is yet."

"You might want to look at people in our year with dark hair," I said, suddenly recalling Celine's statement in Rathbone's classroom.

"What makes you say that?"

"That's what Celine remembered. That someone with dark hair attacked her."

"And your year because all the other incidents happened to students in your year?"

I nodded. I guess he was an enforcer for a reason: he hadn't missed the connection.

"It's not much to go on, but it's better than nothing. But we're going to need to find Dominic first."

"Let me help. I know he doesn't like me and has probably been trying to find a way to find me guilty, but that doesn't mean I want anything bad to happen to him."

Zachary nodded and knelt down, then whispered something in his familiar's ear I couldn't catch. It sounded distinctly non-English. The creature vanished, leaving me and Zachary standing by the gate. "Okay, we'll go look for him, but if things get too dangerous, I want you to back off."

I laughed. "Make up your mind, already. I can't be both the damsel in distress and the warrior princess fighting for my own freedom."

He laughed, too. "You're right. You can fight with the best of them. I guess part of me just wants to protect you."

"Because you think you're stronger than me?" I raised an eyebrow, even though I knew he was far stronger than I could ever hope to be.

"Because I care too much about you to see you get hurt."

I smiled. I liked his answer much better than mine. "So, where do we start?"

"We retrace his steps."

That meant heading to the canteen. It would be bustling with students and staff right about now. That also meant I had a high likelihood of finding the one person who would be more than willing to go digging for information for me without asking questions. And for once, I didn't mean my best friend.

I led the way across the courtyard, past the tree Eva and I had spent a considerable amount of our first year hanging out under, and back into the foyer of the academy. I would have expected other people to be milling about, but the corridor leading to the canteen was empty. Most of them were too busy studying, I guessed. I could hear the noise of dozens of people eating and talking coming through the door to the canteen, though. That was a good sign.

I stopped Zachary short of following me in. "People are going to think it's weird us walking around together and questioning people. Someone might assume something's wrong and go off telling Bevan. I'm guessing he wouldn't be so inclined to wait and see if Dominic turns up sometime tomorrow with a hangover."

"You're probably right." He reached out and grabbed my arm. "But I'm fairly certain he's not in there. My familiar told me he'd been last seen here, but that was hours ago."

"I'm not here looking for him," I answered, and eased

myself free of his grip.

I slipped into the canteen, pausing to grab a protein bar and stow it in my back pocket as I scanned the room. I wasn't entirely certain the person I was looking for would be present, but my heart leapt in relief when I spotted Belinda sitting at a table in the far corner, her nose in a book. I hated to pull her away from cramming for exams, but she'd been eager to ply me with information before. Hopefully she'd be happy to help again.

Sliding into the seat opposite her, I cast a shadow over her reading material. She looked up, momentary annoyance replaced instantly by excitement. "Norah. Hi!"

"Hi, Belinda. Sorry to bother you. I know you're probably cramming. Exams are the worst."

"I like tests," she said, and then immediately looked startled by her own admission, ducking her head as her cheeks flushed pink.

"Cool," I said cheerfully, because I needed her to open up to me, not to sit wishing the ground would open up on her. "That makes precisely one of us, but maybe you'll rub off on me."

She lifted her head. "I'm kind of really good at them. When I was younger, I got teased about it. Until other kids realised I could help them do better."

"Wish you'd been here last year. My botany grade

would have been higher."

"I could probably help you with that," she said and set her book aside.

I waved her offer away. "Thanks, but I'll figure it out." Or, more likely, I wouldn't. But that wasn't our biggest concern right now. "Anyway, the reason I came looking for you is because I need some help."

Her eyes widened and she quickly slammed her book shut. "Sure, what's going on?"

The canteen might be noisy, but that didn't mean that people couldn't overhear us. I really didn't need the wrong person catching wind of what I was asking her and spreading it round the whole academy. Plus, even though I trusted Belinda to go digging for me and report back, I wanted to make sure Eva was in on this, too. As I'd learned the hard way last year, having my best friend in on the plans tended to have better results. Also, I got less beat up that way.

"Not here," I answered Belinda. "It's... sensitive."

Belinda nodded with such vigour she was in danger of giving herself whiplash. She grabbed her bag and tossed her book in before following me out. Zachary waited dutifully by the door and Belinda baulked at the sight of him.

"It's okay. He's with us."

Her eyes looked like they were about to pop right out

of her face, so I pressed on quickly.

"He knows what's going on. In fact, he's part of why what I need to ask you is so sensitive," I said. "Come on, this way."

I turned without giving her chance to freak out, and strode purposefully in the direction of the library. After a second, I heard her rapid footsteps catching up with me, and hid my smile. Behind us, Zachary's heavier footsteps followed at a measured pace. He was obviously trying not to freak her out more than his very existence already had, for which I was eternally grateful. Or would be, if we didn't end up at war with each other by this time tomorrow.

"Is this about the attack?" she whispered.

I twisted round to eye Zachary.

"Not exactly," he answered.

I rolled my eyes at him and tried to convey exactly how unhelpful that answer was. He cleared his throat.

"I'm going to check a few other places," he said. "Do what you need, and I'll meet you at Valentine's Day."

He turned on his heel and strode off in the opposite direction to where I thought I could make out a flash of translucent yellow-brown fur. I dedicated a couple of seconds to checking out his backside.

"He does know Valentine's Day was months ago, right?" Belinda said uncertainly as we walked, probably concerned that our new and somewhat imposing-looking ally had lost all touch with reality.

"Uh, it's complicated," I said. Zachary had spoken in code for a reason, and whilst I thought he was probably being overly cautious, he was right about one thing—we didn't know who we could trust, not really, and it didn't pay to chance being overheard.

We found Eva at the same table she'd been at the other day. This time she didn't bother hiding the books of photos she'd been poring over.

"I need your help," I said without preamble. The library was deserted, with most of the students presumably studying in their room—or not at all, having decided that if they hadn't learned it by now, they weren't going to.

"Everything okay with you and Celine?" She set the books aside and pivoted in her seat. Her eyes snagged on Belinda for a moment before moving on to me.

"Not really. Though she put on a good show for Rathbone until we got out of earshot. Anyway, that's not what I need help with. One of the druids has gone missing."

"Zachary?"

"No, the other one. Dominic. He hasn't been seen for a few hours. I told Zachary I'd help look for him, but it's a big academy. I could use a little help asking around. And honestly, the two of you questioning people isn't going to arouse nearly as much suspicion as me doing it."

"Hang on, why are you helping look for the druid?" Belinda's tone was all righteous indignation. "Everyone knows he thinks you are behind the attack."

"It's his job to investigate anyone who he thinks is guilty. I'm not a fan of being his number one suspect, trust me, but I'm not above the law, and nor should I be. And all of that aside, a druid enforcer going missing in our academy looks bad for everyone."

I hesitated. I could leave it at that and have a clear conscience that I'd told her everything she needed to know. But if I wanted her to trust me, then I had to be trustworthy. Ah, hell, in for a penny, in for a pound.

"Zachary is a friend, and he needs my help with this."

Belinda's mouth opened into a wide 'o' shape. "Something happened between you on Valentine's Day, didn't it?"

My cheeks warmed at the memory. "It did. And look, maybe if I can help find Dominic, it'll go some way to clearing my name."

"I'll ask around and see if I can find anything out," she said, just about stopping short of giving me a salute.

"Thanks. I really appreciate knowing I have people who have my back around here."

"We'll find him. And I know you'll be cleared. I just

know it."

She hurried off, leaving me and Eva alone in the library. I sank into the seat beside her and narrowed my eyes at the first year's retreating back, Zachary's unspoken warning racing through my mind. "You don't think she's the one going after people on my behalf, do you?"

Eva snorted. "No way. She's way too in awe of you to do anything that might piss you off. And I reckon attacking people might do just that."

"Yeah, you're probably right." I glanced at the pile of books spread out on the table. "Any luck hunting for your dad?"

"Not as such, no. I know I should be studying." She rubbed at her temples. "I'm pretty sure my grades are going to suck this year. But if I can just find some lead to who he is and track him down, it will be worth it."

"You'll sort it. I have faith in you," I said, leaning over to give her a one-armed hug. I plucked the protein bar from my back pocket and deposited on the table in front of her. "And in the meantime, you can eat something and help me find this missing druid."

"Yeah, okay." She stretched her shoulders out with an audible click. "I could use the break."

I helped her packed up the books and we dropped them in the dorm before heading off in opposite directions to see who we could find. I doubted I personally would have any luck, but that didn't mean I wasn't going to try. As I wandered the corridors, talking to the few students I saw and getting nothing but weird looks for my troubles, I noticed the many runes that lined the walls and floor, tucked discreetly into the stonework. The corrupt druid enforcer, Seneca, had placed runes around the academy last year as part of her plan to tamper with our magic, but these looked older, faded.

"Hey." Reggie's voice caught me off guard as I bent to study a series of newer looking markings along the wall in one of the second-floor corridors. They looked like they represented concealment and deflection. "What are you doing?"

"Uh, nothing," I mumbled. The light glinted off the runes, making it appear as though they glowed in the dim corridor.

"Looks like you were staring at the wall pretty intently. Trying to open a portal in it and escape from exams?"

I laughed awkwardly. "Ha, I wish. Just, well, have you ever noticed just how many runes there are everywhere in this place?"

"I'm not sure if you've noticed, Norah," he said with a grin, "but this is a magic academy. They've got to keep us safe, right?"

"Yeah, I suppose." I brushed the thoughts of the

runes aside. I doubted Reggie would have seen Dominic, but it was worth asking. "Hey, I've got sort of an odd question for you if you've got a minute."

He shrugged. "Sure."

He was being much more attentive to me than he had in weeks. Maybe I'd just caught him in a good mood.

"You know the druids who've been hanging around," I began.

"You mean the ones hovering over us when they aren't wanted?"

"Those would be the ones, yes. The taller one with the angry face. You haven't seen him around today, have you?"

Reggie scratched at his chin. "I might have noticed him loitering around the canteen this morning but haven't seen him since. Why? Do you think they've gone off and finally decided to leave us all be?"

"Doubtful," I answered.

"Why are you so interested in the whereabout of the druids, then?" he pressed.

"Well, you might have noticed," I said, mimicking his earlier tone and smile, before getting serious, "I'm not exactly their favourite person. I prefer to keep an eye on them. To make sure they're not trying to stitch me up."

He seemed to buy that response. "Well, if I happen to notice them hanging around the girls' dorms, I'll be sure to let you know."

Before I could question why *he* would be hanging around the girls' dorms to see someone else hanging around there, he shoved his hands into his pockets and started looking down the corridor the way I'd come. "I should get going. Need to get in some last-minute Energy Manipulation practice. You want to join me?"

I should be studying, and practice wasn't a bad idea, but I needed to meet up with Zachary, Belinda, and Eva to see if they'd found anything. And really, if I hadn't got it by now, what difference was an extra hour going to make?

"I promised Eva I'd study with her," I said, grateful he didn't have her magic for telling a lie. "It's kind of our end-of-semester things. Girls' night in cramming to the small hours."

His face fell slightly. "Right. Well, guess I'll see you for exams, then. Good luck."

"Thanks. You, too. See you around."

I waited until he was gone before heading for the first floor and the alcove Zachary and I had occupied. He was waiting for me. His familiar was nowhere to be seen, but I spotted Belinda and Eva walking up from the opposite end of the corridor.

"Any luck?" I asked once we were all gathered.

"No one's seen him since breakfast," Belinda said.

"One girl I talked to said she thought she saw him heading off grounds, but she couldn't be sure."

"Same," Eva said. "I talked to a couple of people who saw him in the canteen this morning. Mentioned something about piling two plates high with food."

"He does like to eat," Zachary said. "And if I'm being honest, he has pulled a disappearing act before on our last assignment."

"You could have mentioned that before," I snapped.

"That time, he was sneaking off to see a girl he'd met. But she's in another country and I don't know if he's still seeing her."

"He could have portalled out to her though, right?" I said, because I was pretty confident that druids couldn't qualify as enforcers without mastering that particular skill.

"That's true," Zachary agreed reluctantly. "I don't want to get him in trouble, but if he has just gone off to hook up with someone, I wish he'd have told me. Then I could have at least covered for him."

"You said you could hold off until tomorrow evening to report him missing?"

"No longer than that. We have to report in every couple of days with any progress. Any later than tomorrow and my superiors will get suspicious."

"Okay, well look, we have exams all day tomorrow, but once they're over, we can keep looking for him. Make a list of any friends he might have gone to see, and since we'll have more freedom once exams are done, we can go looking off grounds if we need to."

"Sounds good to me," Belinda said, casting a furtive glance at the alcove then looking from me to Zachary. She was probably trying to figure out just what had transpired in the small space. I hated to tell her it had been one kiss and he hadn't talked to me for weeks afterwards. "Maybe we'll get lucky. He might have just gone off to drown his sorrows about not being able to find the *real* culprit."

I hid another smile at her protective tone. It really was good to know someone else had my back round here.

Zachary shook his head and gave a sad smile. "If we're lucky. I'd have to give him a talking to but I wouldn't have to let our superiors know. I hope that's the case."

"Okay. You should all get back to your studies," Zachary said, and pulled me aside as the other two left. "It's probably safer if it's just the two of us. I know they can probably hold their own, at least, I know Eva can, but I don't want to put anyone else in danger. If I thought I could get away with it, I'd tell you to sit it out, too. But I'm willing to bet that's a battle I'm not going to win."

"And you'd be right. I'll meet you back here after my exams tomorrow. We'll get this sorted. I want him found just as much as you do."

The thought did cross my mind that whoever had attacked Celine might have gone after Dominic. He had been the one leading the interrogations of the students and staff and it was possible the assailant thought he was more of a threat. But, even if that were the case, it didn't bring me any closer to finding him. It wasn't like I had the first idea who was behind it all—dark haired and probably in my year was hardly much of a criminal profile.

But I'd have to put that thought on ice for the next twenty-four hours, because if I failed all my exams and got expelled, I wasn't going to be finding anyone. Maybe I should go find Reggie and take him up on that Energy Manipulation practice after all.

Chapter Twenty-One

I didn't manage to find Reggie to take him up on that practice offer, but Eva stayed up late with me trying to figure out how exactly we were going to pass Rathbone's exam. By the afternoon of the following day, I was exhausted and I knew I still had Runes and Energy Manipulation to go. At least Instructor Glover's exam had been easy.

I bid Eva farewell as she headed off for her extra botany exam and settled in for Runes. I'd been keeping an eye out as I moved around during the morning, hoping I'd see Dominic scowling at me so we'd know that he was okay and we didn't have to worry. But no such luck. True, I'd spent most of the day in exams, but if he'd surfaced, I was sure Zachary would have found a way to let me know. I pushed the thought aside as the last few students trickled in. I needed to focus if I wanted to earn a pass on my remaining two exams.

"You ready?" I asked Reggie as he slunk into his seat in front of me just before Rathbone closed the door to the lecture room.

Reggie turned to look at me and I spotted dark circles under his eyes. He looked less enthused than he had last night, and I could see the worry lines wrinkling his forehead.

"Just want to get it done with," he murmured and turned back to the front of the room.

Rathbone had already explained that the exam would be interpreting a series of runes and explaining what they did in a practical sense. If we chose to take the advanced course next semester, we'd actually get to use them ourselves.

I'd come into this exam feeling confident. I just seemed to *get* runes. I tried not to look too eager as Rathbone passed out the exam papers. I knew I could finish the test in half the allotted time and still get a decent score. But there was a whole saying about pride coming before a fall, so I buried my cockiness, and set about answering the fifty questions slowly and methodically.

I wrote more than was necessary in the explanation of what the rune combinations did, and I may even have gushed a little about one particular combination on question forty-six about defensive circles. I'd never imagined a series of drawn symbols could be... elegant.

In front of me, I could hear Reggie scribbling across his own paper at a fever pace. Maybe he was angling to finish before me so that people couldn't say I was such a show-off. Maybe he was just better than me. I tried to block out his rapid-fire pace as I studied the final few questions. They were no doubt supposed to get more complex as we went on, but these seemed easier than the ones at the start of the exam. There were fewer runes to decipher, for one thing. The images almost seemed to come alive and jump off the page, dancing in front of my eyes as I wrote down their meanings. *Deflection. Concentration.*

Those two didn't seem to go together at first. I sat there staring at the page for a solid five minutes, not writing anything. The grumbles and scratching of pens on paper around me became ambient white noise as I tried to figure out how this would work. Maybe I was overthinking it. It was probably possible to concentrate a deflection rune on a very specific point, almost like a beam that no one could cross. So, I scribbled that down as my answer and moved on.

The last couple questions seemed to at least make sense and I was able to answer them in far more detail. I was about to start back to the one where I'd scribbled the half-arsed answer when Rathbone's voice cut through my focus.

"Ten minutes left."

I still couldn't think of a good way to beef up that answer, no matter how hard I tried, so I ended up leaving it. I'd answered the other forty-nine questions well enough that one weak answer shouldn't cost me much. I stayed in my seat until Rathbone called time and then followed Reggie up to deposit my answer sheet on Rathbone's desk before leaving the room. We'd be back in there in fifteen minutes for Energy Manipulation.

I scanned the people milling about the corridor, hoping to spot Eva. She was good at botany, but she'd been worried about her exam, anyway. That was just who she was. It was probably why she had a habit of acing exams—she constantly convinced herself she needed to know more than she did. Of course, she hadn't had as much time to study as usual, what with devoting so much time to trying to track down her father. So she only put in about ten times the hours I did. Still plenty good enough for a pass, I was sure.

She was nowhere to be seen, and I almost ran straight into Celine, flanked by Miranda and Jessa, a little way up the corridor. She glared at me, flipped her bright red hair over one shoulder and turned away. At least she seemed to be back to her old self. *Joy, oh joy.*

"How'd your exam go?" Eva's voice came from my right, and I spun to find my friend standing there.

"Pretty easy. Well, there was one question that kind of stumped me. But I think I'll score well enough to get a decent grade. How was advanced botany?"

"Brutal." She held up a bandaged hand. "The plants got a little aggressive. I think I was probably a bit careless, too."

"Ouch. Are you going to be okay for Energy Manipulation, or do you need to go to the medwing?"

"I'll be fine. I don't want to bother the healers, it'll fix itself in a day or two."

I reached over to give her a hug. Rory stood against the opposite wall, his big frame casting a shadow along the floor. He eyed me and I didn't even try to hide my annoyance. "Do you have something to say, Rory?"

He shook his head. "Nope. Just trying to remember how the hell I'm supposed to separate magic from my body."

I snorted. "Yeah, well, you aren't alone there."

"Just try not to get anyone else hurt," he muttered and pushed himself off the wall.

I blew out a breath. I wasn't going to engage in the blame game. I had enough trouble getting my head straight for Energy Manipulation.

"He knows we're going to be in little rune protected spaces, right?" Eva said, shaking her head in irritation.

Rathbone appeared and opened the door to the classroom.

"Second year Energy Manipulation, come in, please."

"Here goes nothing," I murmured to Eva as we filed into the room. The desks had been all pushed to the perimeter of the room. I claimed a spot all the way in the back corner. I know people wouldn't actually be able to see me one way or another once we got started, but it made me feel better. I was nervous enough about flunking without worrying about people watching me do it, even if those worries were completely unfounded.

I caught Celine claiming a spot as far away from me as possible—presumably in case I somehow 'stole' her magic again. Jessa and Miranda took the spaces on either side of her, and Eva found a spot in the middle of the room as Rory trudged to the back row in the corner opposite mine. The rest of the class shuffled in and I spotted Reggie race in at the last minute, claiming the only spot available—right by the door.

"You all know the exam topic already," Rathbone said. "You will create an energy shield and detach it from your bodies. Given the confines of the exam space, you won't be expected to project it anywhere, but you will need to sustain the shield around you for at least a minute to receive a passing grade."

Before anyone could protest, the magical barriers went up around us, blocking out our view of everyone else in the room, Rathbone included. I just had to get through this exam and then I'd be able to meet up with Zachary and frankly I didn't think finding an AWOL druid enforcer could be nearly as hard as half a dozen dumb exams crammed into one day. But first I had to manifest a shield and detach it from myself, which I hadn't been able to manage yet, despite all the practicing. Okay, I suppose I hadn't practiced quite as much as I could—and should—have. Oh well, too late to do anything about it now.

I closed my eyes, running through one of the breathing exercises Glover had taught us in Unique Magics, and tried to let the magic come to me at its own pace. It was there, just out of reach like always.

"Stop fighting it," Zachary's voice echoed in my mind.

I wasn't trying to, but maybe he was right, and deep down, some part of me was scared of my magic, and trying to push it down.

Okay. I could do this. Just… stop fighting. Easy.

As if sensing my newfound determination, my magic ebbed to the surface. I latched on to it, pulling it out of me and channelling it into my hands. It undulated in my hands, and it settled into a sphere shape. Phase one, check. Two more to go.

"You can control it," Zachary's voice egged me on.

He was right. I *could* control it. I could do this. I pulled my hands apart and the sphere elongated and flattened out into something resembling the top of a table. You could probably call it a shield shape, if you kind of squinted. I even managed to turn it so that the flattened part faced away from me. Not that it would do much to protect the rest of me, but beggars couldn't be choosers.

Now the hardest part. The piece I hadn't yet been able to master. Heat prickled along the nape of my neck. This was what he wanted to see if we could do, and I really didn't want to disappoint him. Not after everything he'd done for me.

"The magic wants to be used. It wants to obey you," Zachary's voice came again.

I started at that line. He'd never told me anything like that. Was my mind making stuff up now? Because fantasising encouraging messages from my crush in the middle of an exam was *not* helpful. Well, okay, maybe it was kind of helpful. Imaginary Zachary was right: the magic *did* want to be used. I turned my focus back to the shield I could feel humming with intention, still attached to my hands in front of me.

"Detach," I whispered, but nothing happened.

A loud crack came from behind me, and I jumped. The shield wavered between my hands and my breath caught in my throat. *Don't fade, don't fade.* I was pretty sure I'd never manage to conjure it a second time. The runes in place made it impossible to see what was behind me, but I thought I saw a strange glow emanating from beyond my barrier. Had someone had an accident? *Focus!*

A second boom came from my right, and I tried to

ignore it. It had to be part of the exam. Rathbone's way of testing our focus, or giving us some incentive to hold our shields. Either way, not helpful.

The flashes and sounds continued at odd intervals. My heart was no longer hammering in my throat, but it was still enough to send a pulse of adrenaline through me each time one of the loud bangs sounded—and each pulse of adrenaline made my shield flare brighter and flicker unpredictably. Tiny little pinpricks jabbed all over my arms, trying to claw at me. The shield, which somehow hadn't vanished yet, grew in size until it was as tall as me.

It's coming from behind.

I turned my palms outward and pushed. To my surprise, the shield came away from my fingers and hovered in the air in front of me before wrapping around me to ward off whatever attack was coming my way. The crashes and booms continued, and I just stood still, waiting for my shield to fade.

It had to have been longer than a minute. Maybe even longer than five or six by the time my shield fell. The barrier around me vanished along with it. Relief and elation flooded through me, leaving me both exhilarated and weak as a day old kitten at the same time. The exam was over.

I grinned over at Eva and gave her a thumbs up. She

nodded, but didn't say anything. She looked as worn out as I felt, which was definitely not normal for her. Maybe her botany-inflicted wound had interfered in her magic casting after all.

"Exam scores will be posted by the end of the week," Rathbone called.

That was our cue to leave. I waited while other students headed out. Reggie was gone like a flash and Celine wasn't far behind him, trailed by her entourage. I fell into step beside Eva.

"I actually did it," I said, failing to hide the excitement in my voice.

"I managed to detach mine, but I'm not sure if it was for the full minute," she said, her brow furrowing. "It seemed like it didn't last long enough. And what the hell were all those sounds?"

"Must have been part of the exam. I felt, like, these weird pinpricks attacking me, and that's when I was able to make the shield do what I wanted. If I'm honest, most of it was Zachary coaching me."

She arched a dark brow at my words. "Say that again?"

"Okay, well not like coaching really. Just I sort of remembered this conversation we had the other day where he was giving me encouragement. I think it helped."

"Speaking of your favourite druid, aren't we supposed to be meeting up with him now?"

I pulled a face. I hadn't exactly told her or Belinda they weren't welcome at my rendezvous with Zachary. "Uh, he kind of told me to show up alone."

"You asked for our help. You can't just kick us out now. Belinda is going to be crushed."

"I know." I winced, and for a moment considered ignoring Zachary's request. It didn't feel right cutting the other two out, even if it was for the best of reasons. But he was right, we couldn't put them in danger. "He's just worried that you'll get hurt and he doesn't want that to happen. And neither do I. Please. Do this for me."

She didn't look impressed. "Fine. But Norah Sheehan, if you get yourself killed, I will find a necromancer to raise your arse so I can tear you a new one, is that clear?"

"Crystal," I said, and fired off a mock salute. "And save me some dinner, 'kay?"

She narrowed her eyes. "I'll bring you some pizza back to the dorm. But if you're not back by midnight, I'm eating it."

"Harsh, but fair," I grinned, and gave her a quick hug before hurrying off down the corridor.

It didn't take me long to reach the spot I'd met Zachary at before. The corridor was empty. And so was the alcove. Was I early?

No, we'd agreed that we'd meet right after the end of my exam. A sinking feeling hit me as I paced, turning at every sound, hoping to see his face. He wouldn't stand me up. Not like this and not about something so important.

Something was wrong.

Chapter Twenty-Two

I tried not to panic as I searched the first-floor corridor. Some of the third years had finished their exams, too, and were milling about. I didn't know any of them and it would seem too out of place for me to ask if they'd seen Zachary.

"Everything all right, Miss Sheehan?" Dean Bevan's voice echoed across the entryway.

Shit. I couldn't risk letting him know that something was wrong. One missing druid we might be able to cover up, but two was another matter. I had to find them, and I had to do it without arousing any suspicion. I swallowed hard and turn to face the dean with what I was certain was a wholly unconvincing smile.

"Uh, yeah. Just trying to de-stress. Exams, you know?"

Bevan's gaze narrowed as he studied me.

"I know we haven't always seen eye to eye, but I am glad I ran into you," he said. He stepped closer, not giving me a chance to duck and run. "I hope you know there's no hard feelings about our last conversation."

I really didn't have time for this. I needed to find Zachary. "Oh, no, I didn't think there were." I glanced around the foyer, hoping I could at the very least pretend to make a beeline for someone else. No one presented themselves.

"You know, I've been hearing good things from your instructors. If you're ever interested, I can talk to the Enforcer Academy and see if that opportunity is still available."

"I'm not sure that's really for me, but thanks." My weight shifted from foot to foot, and I probably looked really shady to anyone else walking by. "Look, thanks for the vote of confidence. I just realised I left something in one of my exam rooms. I better go get it."

I pivoted on my heel and didn't give him chance to speak as I strode away. I passed by the alcove again but it was still empty, and somewhere deep down I knew it would stay that way. Zachary wasn't late. He was missing.

"Hey," Belinda's voice drifted to me from across the corridor.

Clearly Eva hadn't given her the message I'd wanted to meet Zachary solo. Then again, maybe she'd seen something that could be useful.

"Hey," I returned her greeting. "Have you seen Zachary?"

She cocked her head to the side. "Come to think of it, I haven't seen him in a while. I mean, I saw him in the canteen at breakfast but that was it." Her eyes went wide. "Not that I'm keeping tabs on him or anything."

Maybe he was hoping to find Dominic returned for breakfast. But that didn't explain was he was now.

"You're sure you saw him this morning?" I pressed.

"Yeah. He gave me a nod and everything. He seems all right, for a druid."

I chewed at my lip. I was tempted to go hunt down my communication stone and give Kelsey a call to see if she'd heard anything. It was entirely possible he'd found Dominic and just hadn't had time to fill me in. But I still didn't believe he would just disappear on me.

"So, what's the news?" Eva appeared from a nearby staircase.

"Zachary is missing," I replied.

"But I saw him this morning."

"That's what Belinda said," I replied. "Which means he's been missing for hours."

"Maybe he just went to fill his superiors in?" Belinda suggested.

I shook my head. "No, he told me he could hold off until tonight and he meant that. He knows how bad it would look for one of his fellow enforcers to go missing. Enforcers and this academy don't exactly have the best reputation."

Eva nodded. "We could check the medwing. Maybe Dominic was hurt and he took him straight there."

"Maybe. But wouldn't they have called in their own

people? Wouldn't we have heard someone say they'd seen the druid healers back? They're not exactly inconspicuous with all the cloaks and stuff."

They both stared at me in silence. Eventually, I shrugged. The medwing was as good a place to start our search as any. We headed that way and my stomach started doing flips the closer we got there. I didn't much care what happened to Dominic. He'd been kind of an arse to me, and despite what I'd said to Belinda about not wanting to be above the law, he wouldn't be going on my Christmas card list any time soon.

But I couldn't stop picturing Zachary lying in a bed with some grievous injury having tried to defend his fellow druid. Or worse, lying somewhere in the dirt, alone.

My hands shook as I stepped into the space. It was eerily quiet. I expected to be accosted by one of the healers, demanding to know what was wrong with me now. Instead, I spotted Instructor Glover fiddling with some bandages on her forearm. She turned at the sound of my footsteps and embarrassment coloured her cheeks.

"Are you okay?" Surprise muted my terror for a moment, and I canted my head.

"Fine, fine," she answered, dismissing my concern. "Just a bit of an accident during an exam."

"Shouldn't one of the healers be handling that?"

"Not worth bothering them over," she answered, and arched a brow at me. "Why are you here? You don't look to be in need of medical attention. For once."

"I, uh, I was just looking for someone…" I trailed off.

"I'd be happy to help if I knew who you were looking for."

"Uh, one of the druids." She didn't need to know they were both missing.

She deftly pinned one of the bandages in place—not the first time she'd done that—and then returned her attention to me.

"Why are you looking for them?" Her gaze narrowed and I fought to keep my unease in check, and, preferably, off my face. Bloody good question.

"Just trying to see if they've decided to move on from hounding me about the whole Celine thing," I said after a beat. *Real smooth, Norah.* For someone who'd spent a considerable amount of time labelled as a supposed criminal mastermind, I really should be better at lying by now.

"They usually post up in the dean's office. Have you checked there?"

"Uh, no. I'll do that. Good luck with your arm, Instructor."

I turned on my heel and hurried out of the room. So

much for not raising any suspicions. Still, at least Glover only suspected me of being weird, not of covering up two missing druids, so that was kind of a victory.

I found Belinda and Eva waiting for me down the corridor a few paces. I shook my head when I saw them. "Only Glover was in there."

"Is there any other place he might have gone?" Eva asked.

None that I could think of, which was the frustrating part. Maybe a call to Kelsey was a good idea after all. "I've got one other thing I can try but it's a long shot. I'll meet up with you in an hour and if we've found nothing, then I guess we have to go to Bevan and let him know both druids have gone AWOL."

"What do you think he'll do?" Belinda whispered.

I shrugged. "He'll have to report it to the Council. After that, I have no idea." I really hoped it didn't have to go that far, because I was pretty sure the druids had gone to war for less. "In the meantime, can the two of you check the grounds? I can't shake the feeling that... well, we should just try to find him."

I left them to that and headed back toward the dorms. I made it to the second floor when that feeling of being watched crept up my scalp. I turned on the bottom step but saw nothing. I stepped through the doorway into the corridor and collided with something misty, yet oddly solid.

I looked down to find Zachary's familiar prowling in front of me, barring my path. What had he said about the creature? He could be independent from him and didn't have to go where he went. So, Zachary could be off grounds but his familiar could still be present.

"Uh, I have no idea if you can understand me," I began as the creature continued to pace back and forth, its translucent yellow ears pressed slick to its skull—or what would be its skull if it were an actual cat.

It had to understand what I was saying. Zachary spoke to it in English. "I'm looking for Zachary. He was supposed to meet me, but he didn't show up. Do you know where he is?"

The familiar let out an angry silent yowl and pawed at the ground before darting off down the corridor. I guess I was playing a game of chase, whether I wanted to or not. I shouldn't have been surprised the familiar moved like the wind. After all, he was basically air made semi-corporeal.

I ran behind him, but he seemed to be leading me in circles, passing the same staircase where we'd encountered each other. By the fourth time we passed it, I let out a shrill whistle.

"Okay, this clearly isn't working."

The familiar hissed at me, panting as if out of breath.

That didn't seem right. I noticed his whole body quiver as he started forward again. I shuffled to block his path, not that I could really stop a spirit. He could presumably go right through me if he wanted.

"Listen to me," I said, holding my hands palm out so he knew I wasn't trying to threaten him. "I know you're trying to take me to Zachary, but something is interfering with your ability to get to him."

Deflection and Concealment.

Hadn't I seen those runes in one of the corridors around here? It had seemed an odd combination then. And then something similar had come up on Rathbone's exam earlier. I should have realised it meant something. There was no reason for the academy administration to have any sort of deflection runes operating on the grounds; especially not after what happened last year with Seneca. If anything, they should have had Rathbone place more protective runes around the grounds.

"I think I know what's going on," I told the familiar, trying to remain calm. "I need you to let me lead. I think I can figure out what's happened."

I turned and started down the way the creature had taken me four times before. Except this time, I closed my eyes and stood still. The deflection rune often messed with a person's sense of perception. It interfered with what they could see or hear. But I wasn't planning to look with my eyes. I felt my shadows swirl to the surface, ready to be used. To obey me.

Depending on how the runes were enchanted, only certain people or specific magic would be affected. I was sure they'd been active when I noticed them the other day, which made me think that it wasn't meant to keep me out—which was weird. Surely the true culprit wouldn't want me to find them? After all, I was the perfect fall person.

I pushed out with my magic, trying not to see what wasn't there, but to find the magic that was keeping the familiar from finding what it sought. It didn't take me long for my shadows to bump against the power of the rune. Still with my eyes closed, I shuffled closer, letting my magic guide me to the destination.

When I opened my eyes again, I found myself at the patch of wall. The runes pulsed violet and when I pressed a hand to them, they were warm to the touch. Whoever had activated them had done so recently and was pouring a hell of a lot of magic into keep them going.

I wish we'd actually started doing rune construction in a practical way in class. Then I could have undone the magic, or at least tried. I'd have to resort to the cruder method of scratching them out so they didn't work properly. Scouring the area, I finally found a small chunk of stone. I dragged it across the surface of the runes. The purplish hue flickered and eventually died completely. What had looked like empty corridor a moment ago turned into a door.

I was about to tell the familiar to resume its search when it let out a piercing howl and dissipated through the door.

Well, *that* wasn't a good sign.

Everything pointed to Zachary being behind that door along with the answers to all my questions, and the reason he hadn't come to find me.

There was no turning back now.

Chapter Twenty-Three

I shoved the door and tumbled into the hidden room, and the sight stopped me dead in my tracks. In one corner, with his hands shackled to the wall high above his head, was Dominic. He was bruised and bloodied, and if the gods were smiling, only unconscious.

Zachary was slumped over on the floor, wrists chained through some sort of metal ring bolted into the ground. Magic suppressing cuffs dug into his wrists, and I could see the raw skin from where I stood. He gave a soft moan, stifled by the gag in his mouth, and my heart skipped a beat. He was alive.

Curled up at his feet was the familiar, its whole incorporeal body trembling with pain or with fear, I couldn't tell which.

Slowly, Zachary's eyes opened and focused on my face. A small smile quirked his lips upward around the gag before they fell into a frown. He shook his head but didn't try to speak.

"I was wondering when you would get here," a voice called from my right.

I spun to find a single figure standing off to one side, holding a rune etched amulet. Reggie.

And he didn't look like he was part of the rescue

party.

"It was you." My brow furrowed and my heart pounded as the realisation thudded into it. My tongue was heavy in my mouth but the words tumbled out of their own accord. "All the accidents. Celine's attack. It was all you."

He offered a one-shoulder shrug. "To be honest, I'm a little disappointed you didn't realise it sooner, Norah," he said.

I thought back to all the times people around me got hurt. Reggie had been there every time. He was right. I should have seen it sooner.

"You hurt people."

"And I'd do it again!"

A blur of yellow flashed across the room. Reggie spun to it, holding the amulet aloft.

"Piantaich!"

The familiar froze mid-stride, then it flung its head back in a silent scream of agony, and its whole body went into convulsions. Across the room, Zachary let out a roar of fury behind his gag, straining and pulling at his chains in his desperation to get to the creature. Fresh blood seeped from his wrists but he didn't seem to notice.

"You let everyone think it was me," I said loudly, hoping to distract Reggie from his spell. "The druids, Bevan, the whole bloody academy."

He lowered the charm, and the familiar collapsed to the ground, flanks heaving.

"I was going to clear your name," he said, his voice a little uncertain even as he nodded enthusiastically.

"How? By kidnapping the people who were investigating? That just makes me look even guiltier."

"But you don't understand," he said, taking a few steps closer to me.

I fought the urge to back away. The magic he'd cast to keep other people away had been strong. Far more advanced than anything we'd been taught. Which meant he'd done a little self-study. And that made him dangerous. If he didn't believe I was on his side, or at least open to it, I was going to be in a world of hurt. I needed to stall long enough to come up with a plan that didn't end with me six feet under.

"You're right, Reg. I don't understand. Why don't you explain it to me? Tell me why you did all of this."

"For you."

I blinked. "For… me?"

That was when I knew he was crazy. In hindsight, the whole kidnapping two druids and chaining them up in the dungeons thing was probably a clue.

"They shouldn't have treated you the way they did. I had to punish them. To make them pay for hurting you."

"By cursing them? Some people are arseholes, Reggie.

That's life. It doesn't give you the right to hurt them. And if you really knew me, you'd know I never would have wanted someone to do that in my name. So you need to stop now, okay?"

"But I saw what *she* did, how she hurt you."

He didn't need to say Celine's name for me to know he was talking about the redhead. "Yeah, she did. But it wasn't for you to punish her."

He turned his back on me and started pacing. I could see Zachary struggling against his binds. The familiar still lay panting on the ground. I didn't know what Reggie had done to it, or how he'd known how to hurt a noncorporeal being, but at least it was still alive, or existing, or whatever it was. Still, I didn't think I could count on an assist from the creature or its human partner if this got physical.

I really, *really* hoped it didn't get physical.

"We'll fix this," Reggie said abruptly, pivoting on his heel to face me. "We just have to get rid of some loose ends and then we can tell everyone that the investigation's over. The druids couldn't find the culprit and so they… they left."

"Reggie…"

"It'll work." The familiar twitched and Reggie's gaze latched onto it. His expression hardened. "But first I have to take care of that."

He lifted the amulet up high, and Zachary's muted shout burst from behind his gag. His chains rattled as he yanked on them but the ring in the ground didn't budge.

"You want to watch your familiar suffer first, druid?" Reggie said. "The way your kind have made my kind suffer? You want me to torture it?"

Zachary froze, and then shook his head, his eyes silently pleading with the crazed student. Reggie's mouth twisted into a savage smile.

"Stop!" My voice cracked through the air, breathy and desperate. "You don't have to hurt anyone. They'll leave, okay? They'll leave and they won't come back. They won't tell anyone what happened here. It's like you said. They couldn't find the culprit, so they left. That's what they'll tell everyone. So just let them go, okay? Please. This needs to end."

"You're right." He lowered the amulet. "It's time to end this."

He raised his other hand, an energy ball swirling just in front of it. My throat seized up as he pushed it out in front of him, closer to Zachary. Terror flooded me and I choked up the words.

"No, you can't. This has gone too far, you have to stop. For me, Reggie."

He whirled on me, the energy ball freezing mid-air. "Don't you see? I'm doing this for you."

I stepped quickly, putting myself between Zachary and the ball.

"Then don't hurt him. Please. He's my friend."

"Friend? Druids aren't our friends. They're our oppressors."

"He's different. I swear. And all he's done is try to help me. Just…" I swallowed, and forced the words out. "Just like you."

His gaze narrowed, flickering between my face and a spot over my left shoulder. All at once, his features darkened. "He's not your friend. I've seen the way you two sneak around together. Huddling in corners where you think no one's watching. Is that why you rejected me? Because of *him*?"

"No. Reggie, look at me. He's just a friend. I swear."

"Don't lie to me, Norah," he shouted, the energy ball expanding and contracting with the movements of his hands.

"I'm not," I pleaded. "If you care about me at all, Reggie, you'll just let them walk away."

"It's too late for that. You betrayed me. For a filthy druid!" The energy ball flared brightly between us. He sucked in a sharp breath and shook his head. "But I forgive you, Norah. I love you and I know you love me. I don't want to hurt you. But if you side with him, then I'll have to."

I planted my feet and balled my hands into fists at my sides. "Then you're going to have to hurt me."

As last words went, they weren't the worst. Reggie's face contorted in fury and then I could see the energy ball speeding toward me in slow motion. I wanted to close my eyes, so I didn't see it when it hit me, but they were beyond my control.

As if on a puppet string, my arms moved up to chest height and my fingers spread, elongating a shadow shield in a split second. The energy ball hit the shield and fizzled out.

Through the gauzy shimmer of the shield, I caught Reggie's eyes widen in shock. *You and me both.* Before I could work out what to do about my sudden onset of magical talent, paired with the whole avoiding imminent death thing, Reggie snapped another energy ball into existence and threw it at me. I flinched behind my shield, but the wall of shadow engulfed the energy ball and snuffed it out of existence.

Three more energy balls pounded harmlessly against it, like bugs on a windscreen, while I blinked at it in surprise. And then I figured I should probably do something, rather than standing there waiting for it to fail.

"You can't hold that forever, you bitch," Reggie snarled, peppering me with more balls. "But I can keep throwing these all day."

Shit. He was right. On both counts.

A larger ball thwacked into my shield and it flickered, proving his point. But with both hands tied up holding the shield in place, there was no way I could fight back. If I released one of my hands, I was pretty sure the shield would fade.

A series of smaller energy balls formed in Reggie's hands, and he started launching them at the walls. When the first one hit, I expected it to disappear, but it ricocheted and came speeding at my head. I ducked with a yelp, narrowly avoiding being scalped, and spun round to push my shield out just in time to deflect one coming from the other direction.

What the hell use was my shield if he could throw balls *round* it—and where the hell had he learned all this?

"Why. Won't. You. Die?" Reggie screamed as continued to launch balls at me, each more erratic than the one before.

There was a hiss of pain from somewhere behind me and I saw fresh blood leaking from Zachary's arm, and a smouldering patch of material surrounding the wound. I grit my teeth and spun back to Reggie. He was losing control, and if I didn't find a way to stop him soon, it wasn't going to be me who got hurt. It was going to be the person chained to the floor behind me with his magic muted.

Sucking in a deep breath, I commanded the shadows to expand, stretching higher and wider, and spreading into a wide semicircle that protected us both. I felt the magic straining to obey without losing the shield's integrity, and then suddenly little sparks of electricity danced through the black wall, crackling with energy as it bolstered the shadows. I gaped at it. Both my magics, working together. It was beautiful.

And I totally didn't have time to admire it right now. I shook my head and forced myself to focus. Nothing had changed. My magic was holding, for now, but I couldn't keep this up all night, and no-one else knew where we were. There was no way of telling how long it would be until someone discovered the doorway behind the broken rune.

I needed to find a way to fight back. Every part of my being cringed at the idea of using my magic as a weapon. That was how Micah had started, and I didn't dare let myself take even a single step in that direction.

Maybe… maybe there was another way. I didn't need to hurt Reggie, I just needed to stop him throwing magic long enough to restrain him.

Staring at a spot on one side of my shield, I willed it to open, and prayed Reggie was too caught up in his fury to notice the coin-sized hole. Now for the tricky part. I held my breath, and pulled one hand away from the shield, waiting for it to collapse in on me, and the next ball to find its target and for searing pain to claim every inch of my body.

It held.

I moved my hand to the hole, peering through my wall at the crazed student as I took aim, and then commanded my magic.

A shimmering, sparking shadow leapt out like a whip, coiling itself around Reggie's wrists. I pulled tight and it cinched them together, trapping his hands and stopping him forming any more energy balls.

"You shouldn't be able to…" he trailed off.

"Guess we're both full of surprises today."

My shield fell away until it was a shadowy mist drifting around my feet, and I channelled the energy into the coil of shadows binding Reggie's wrists. He snarled and struggled, fighting to get loose.

"It's over, Reggie."

"No, it's not. *Dì-làraich!*"

Tiny tendrils of energy leapt from nowhere at his command, racing up my shadow rope towards me. Panic took over and I disconnected from it with a sharp pang. My magic and his snapped back at him, smashing into his body and hurtling him back. He crashed into the wall with a loud thud and hit the ground. Around him, the floor sparked and crackled with residual energy as it faded. He lay still, unmoving, and nausea doubled me over. I'd done that to him. My magic. I hadn't meant to, I'd just wanted to stop him, but—

His chest rose as his body drew in a shallow breath. He was alive. I hadn't killed him. Relief made me dizzy, and I swayed on my feet, staring blankly at his unconscious body.

Behind me, Zachary groaned, snapping me out of my trance. I hurried over to him, my eyes racing all over his body searching for new injuries, but there were none, save the small wound to his arm from Reggie's badly aimed energy ball. I fumbled with his gag until I found a clasp behind his head keeping it in place. With shaking hands, I pulled it off and tossed it aside.

Before he could speak, I pressed a kiss to his lips.

"Don't scare me like that again," I said.

"Just friends, huh?" he said.

"Tease me later. I need to get you loose before he wakes up." I looked at the cuffs around his raw and bleeding wrists. "How do I get them off?"

Zachary gestured to Reggie's prone form. "He's got a key. Front left pocket."

Of course he does.

If I went ferreting through his pockets, there was a chance it would rouse him. But it was a chance I would have to take. I wasn't going to just sit by while Zachary suffered. I took a tentative step towards him, watching the steady rise and fall of his chest, and then screwed my hands into balls and hurried over to him. I crouched next to his prone form, rooting through his pocket, not daring to look away from his face.

Got it. My fingers closed around the key and I carefully worked it loose, then hurried back over to Zachary.

"Hold still," I said as I jammed the key into the cuff on his right wrist. His jaw clenched and then the cuff popped open, and I ripped it off. The other came away just as easily, and I dropped them both to the floor, with the heavy iron chain still linking them. If I never saw a suppressor cuff again, it would still be too soon.

With the cuffs off, Zachary sat up straighter. Fresh blood leaked from a wound on his temple, and his face was a mess of dirt and bruises, but he didn't seem to notice. He cast around, and then lurched to his feet and snatched up the fallen amulet from the ground. He muttered a word, too quiet for me to hear, then dropped the amulet back to the floor and crushed it under his heel.

Across the room, the familiar drew in a deep, shuddering breath, and Zachary rushed to his side, swaying unsteadily as he dropped into a crouch and held his hands above the creature. Yellow energy pulsed from his palms, and after a few taut seconds, the lynx began to stir. Zachary rocked back on his heels, sweat trickling down his forehead.

"Will he be okay?" I asked.

Zachary nodded. "He was weakened by the amulet, but he'll recover. I'll feed him as much of my magic as I can."

"Sit," I insisted, pressing down on his shoulder. There was almost no resistance before he plopped onto the floor. "You're going to be no use to him if you kill yourself first."

Zachary nodded in acknowledgement.

"He found me," I said. "He knew you needed help."

"You were brilliant," he said, giving me a grateful smile.

"You would have figured out a way out of it without me," I said, feeling the first traces of heat colouring my cheeks.

"I was powerless once he got the cuffs on. And in case no one's told you, trying to cast magic with a head wound is not a lot of fun."

"How did you find him?"

"He came up to me in the canteen this morning and said he needed to talk to me about the investigation. I figured maybe he knew something about Dominic."

"Turns out you were right," I said, gesturing to the unconscious man on the other side of the room.

"He jumped me as soon as I saw Dominic chained up."

He held out his hands, and sent another wave of energy pulsing over his familiar.

"And he really thought the two of you wouldn't find a way to escape?"

Zachary shook his head. "He spelled Dominic to keep him unconscious. I don't think he'd really thought this far ahead. Dominic must have found something out about him and come looking for him alone. Idiot."

I glanced over at the other druid and could see that he was pale, but his chest rose and fell in shallow breaths.

"And, honestly, no, I don't think Reggie was worried about escape," Zachary continued. "He'd warded the door so it only opened for him."

"And me," I noted.

"And you," he agreed. "How did you know where to look?"

"I spotted the magic he'd used to cover this room up the other day. I should have known something was off when he just showed up behind me. But I didn't. I didn't think he was capable of something like this."

"You said he didn't know you very well. Seems like you didn't know him, either."

"And maybe if I had gotten to know him, he wouldn't have gone on some crusade in the name of my honour."

But what Reggie had wanted from me romantically wasn't something I was ever going to give him. Even if Zachary hadn't been in the picture, I wasn't in a place where I wanted a guy who was *that* into me. Dealing with Belinda's worship was all I could tolerate.

"You know, I really was in a bad spot. He was going to kill me until you showed up."

"Guess I'm a hero. Dammit." I jutted my chin toward Dominic. "We should probably get you both to the infirmary to be checked out."

"Yeah."

I offered him my hand and pulled him to his feet, watching him from the corner of my eye when he swayed slightly. The familiar rose to its feet beside him, taking a few uncertain steps.

"Go," Zachary told his noncorporeal partner. "Tell the Circle what happened here, and then return to Tàthadh and rest."

The familiar eyed him for a moment, and I didn't have to be a druid to recognise his concern for Zachary. How intelligent were these spirits?

"I'll be fine. Now go."

The familiar twitched its short tail in agitation, then spun on the spot and disappeared into nothingness. I stared at the spot where he'd been for a moment, then snapped out of it and hurried over to Dominic, rattling his chains as I searched for a way to release them, but they were linked to his suppressor cuffs.

"I'll get the key," Zachary said, and made for his own abandoned cuffs.

Electricity crackled through the air, and I spun to find Reggie on his feet with an energy ball aimed right at my chest.

"You should have paid better attention in class," he said with a sneer, and nodded at my feet.

I glanced down to see the floor beneath me covered in little glowing violet etchings. I tried to call my magic to me, but it felt further away than ever. Suppressing runes. Shit.

"You betrayed me after everything I did for you," he said. "And now you're going to pay for it."

He drew the energy ball back, and then a ball of yellow air smashed into his chest, hurling him back into the wall. His energy ball fizzled out of existence, and Reggie slumped to the ground. Zachary stalked towards him, face dark with fury, and another swirling yellow ball of compressed air formed in his hand. He raised his arm, and it wasn't until he took aim at Reggie's face that I realised what he intended.

"Stop!" I shouted.

I rushed forward, half expecting the runes to hold me back, but it seemed they were only charged to suppress magic, not restrain people.

Zachary turned to look at me, but his aim stayed locked onto the unconscious student.

"What the hell is wrong with you?" I snapped, glaring at him.

"I can't let him hurt you." Zachary's words were thick with emotion.

"He won't," I said. "Now remember who the hell you are—because this isn't it. You're supposed to be the law—not *above* the law."

He swallowed hard and dropped his arm, crushing the ball from existence. He dragged his hand across his face, wincing as he came up against the open wound.

"You're right. I'm sorry." His face paled as he looked at the unconscious student he'd been on the brink of killing, and then he squared his jaw. "Grab those cuffs. I'll secure him and then we can get them both some medical attention."

I wasn't sure I'd go quite *that* far. Frankly, I was in no hurry to see either Reggie or Dominic revived, but I retreated long enough to grab the cuffs from where they lay abandoned on the floor.

Zachary held his hand out for the cuffs, but I simply pulled out the key and tossed it to him, and crouched down beside Reggie. This whole thing had been about me. It was only right that I be the one to finish it. And then I could get on with working out how to actually stay out of trouble for once.

As I secured the second cuff on Reggie's wrist, footsteps pounded down the corridor outside of the room. When I looked up, Eva, Belinda, and Instructor Glover stood there gaping at me.

I glanced at Zachary. "Guess we've got some explaining to do."

Chapter Twenty-Four

"I still can't believe Reggie was behind it all," Eva said two days later as we grabbed breakfast. We hadn't had much chance to speak about things, since the healers had insisted on me staying in the infirmary for observation, despite not having a scratch on me.

"He seemed so harmless," Belinda agreed. If anything, her hero worship had gone up a notch, but I figured letting her spend some time around me was the fastest way to show her I was just an ordinary person, and a screw up at that. Besides, if I flunked any of my exams and got held back a year, I was going to need a friend in all my lectures.

I shook my head and tossed my toast uneaten back onto my plate.

"The signs were all there, but none of us saw them. I was too busy fighting with Celine to see where the real danger was."

"But she's been awful to you all year," Belinda said.

She wasn't wrong—Celine had kicked the crap out of me more than once, but I was the one who'd allowed it to blind me to all other possibilities. And people had almost lost their lives because of it.

"What do you think will happen to him?" she asked

after a long moment. I glanced at Eva, and she shrugged. She was right: Belinda wasn't a kid who needed to be protected from the truth.

"Zachary's superiors took him back to the Circle for sentencing. Given how serious the attacks were, he thinks they'll send him to Daoradh."

"The high security druid prison?" Belinda's eyes were wide as saucers, and I tried not to think of Micah rotting away in the same place. "For how long?"

I shook my head. "Only the council knows that. But he went after two enforcers. I don't think they're going to let him off lightly."

And it was hard to feel bad for him about that. It wasn't just that he'd attacked Zachary, and it definitely wasn't that he'd drugged Dominic, it was the pleasure he'd taken in doing it. He'd gloated while he'd threatened to torture Zachary's familiar, and he hadn't hesitated to try to kill me when I rejected him. He was dangerous, and whilst I was under no delusions that prison would rehabilitate him, it would at least keep everyone safe.

"Speaking of certain enforcers he went after," Eva began, "I hear Zachary refused to leave your side after it happened, even to get medical treatment."

I blushed and hid behind my mug of coffee. "He said he didn't want me to face the music on my own."

He'd insisted on coming with me to Bevan's office,

and no-one had dared argue with him. Then he'd given Bevan a full brief of what had happened, which only required the occasional grunt of agreement from me, and by the time he'd finished, another contingent of enforcers had shown up to take things in hand. Zachary had spoken for me again—and for once I didn't object—and they'd accepted his word without question. I got the sense he might be getting a promotion out of this. Or at least a raise. And it had only required a psychotic stalker bent on becoming some sort of avenging angel for my honour. Easy.

"Does this mean we'll have druids patrolling the halls again next year?"

I shook my head. "I don't think so. He explained it was just one student, working alone."

Belinda shivered. "It's scary to think that one guy could cause so much harm."

We ate in silence for a while, and then I saw clusters of students getting up to leave.

"Results must be up," Eva said, abandoning her almost empty mug. "Are you ready?"

I waved her off. "You go on without me. I'll check mine once the crowds have died down."

She led Belinda away, and once they were out of sight, I slunk off to hide in the library for a while, relieved to get away from the stares of the rest of the students. I really had done a terrible job of blending in this year. I was going to have to work on that.

I holed up at a table and passed an hour or so enjoying the solitude—and bracing myself for this evening's trip back to my home.

"Scared you've failed everything?" Celine's voice caught me off guard and I sat up, my hands balling into fists through instinct.

For once, she wasn't flanked by her lackeys. I didn't respond to her question, and she pouted.

"I've passed everything, no thanks to... well, someone messing with my magic." She held up a hand and sparks jumped from finger to finger.

"Guess Rathbone was right—you didn't lose it completely. And would it kill you to acknowledge it wasn't me that hurt you?"

She pressed a hand to her chest. "It just might."

"What do you want, Celine?" I sighed.

She gestured around our empty surroundings. "I would think the hero would want to be among the throngs getting adoration heaped upon her."

"I'm no hero. And I don't want their praise or their attention. If you and your friends hadn't been such vindictive bitches, then maybe Reggie wouldn't have attacked you, did you ever think of that? If you'd just left me alone, he wouldn't have gone after you and the druids wouldn't have come and made things worse."

"I didn't…" she trailed off. "Maybe a little."

"No, Celine. You took every opportunity to make my life hell. You sent me to the infirmary multiple times for literally no reason. I told you over summer that I'm sorry you went to prison, but I put my neck on the line practically blackmailing the Council to go easy on you. To consider what you did in stopping Seneca. That's all I could do and frankly, I was surprised they listened to me. But your drama isn't my fault."

She stood there like a fish caught on a line for a minute. "I guess I was a little harsh," she replied.

"How about you do us both a favour and we just agree to avoid each other as much as possible next year?"

"Fine," she said before spinning on her heel and leaving me alone.

I didn't believe for a second that she would keep to that, but I had made the effort to put things behind us and move forward. We couldn't both be blinded by our hatred of each other forever, and that meant I had to change how I handled things.

The door to the library opened and closed, and from my vantage point I saw Eva walk in. She headed straight for my table.

"Everyone's cleared out now if you want to check your results," she said.

"You mean you didn't check for me?" I feigned being wounded. Or at least, it was mostly feigned. She could have put me out of my misery just a little early.

"You should see for yourself," she answered.

That piqued my curiosity and I left her alone—likely to keep digging for her father—and headed to the lecture room corridor. As she'd said, there weren't any other people. Not even the instructors were hanging around. I checked the classes I had less confidence in—hey, I'd actually gotten a higher mark in botany this year than last—before moving down to Unique Magics and Energy Manipulation. Glover had apparently been generous with everyone because I had a much higher mark than last year, even though I didn't think I'd progressed enough to warrant it. One down, one to go…

"So, let me guess," Zachary's voice said from behind me. "You aced them."

"I, uh, haven't found my name yet," I said without looking at him. If I did, he'd see the horrific blush that had come over me from head to foot.

I felt his presence behind me as he ran one finger down the list on Energy Manipulation, settling on my name. "Well, look at that, high marks." His breath tickled my ear as he spoke.

"You and Eva set this up, didn't you?"

"Guilty. I have to say, she's quite good at being

sneaky."

"Must be part of her lie detector powers," I replied.

"Even if she helped me orchestrate this little rendezvous, I wanted to talk to you without the mob scene. I'm sorry I didn't manage to get back to see you yesterday. I had to take care of things with the council."

If I turned around now, we would be nose to nose. Among other things, that thought both excited and terrified me. I should ask about Reggie and diffuse the tension. Or at least convert it into something less charged. I should have done a lot of things, but I didn't listen to my brain. I turned and there he was, and he leaned in and kissed me gently on the lips.

"Took you long enough," I said when he pulled back.

"Been a bit busy. Trying to stop crises at this academy. Seems like every time I want to spend time with this girl I fancy, crazy people get in the way."

Couldn't argue with that. "How's Dominic?"

"Recovering. The healers here were able to bring him out of the enchanted sleep Reggie had put him under. His head's a bit fuzzy but he definitely remembers confronting Reggie and then being hit with the spell."

"I still can't believe he did all of this because he wanted to impress me."

"Teenage boys do stupid things for love. As a former teenage boy, I can attest to that from experience."

"Yeah, but he wasn't in love with me. He was infatuated. It's not the same thing."

"Some people have a hard time telling the difference."

I turned back to the exam results and double checked my Energy Manipulation score. Yep, I'd definitely passed. Desperate for a change of subject, I said, "Looks like I'll be around for one last year. I might even make it to graduation at this rate."

"I never had a doubt," he said with a smile, and brushed a lock of hair out of my face.

"I still don't get why everything seemed so easy when I was fighting Reggie. I mean, I've never even done the whole shield thing before that day and to sustain it and hold him off, that should have been more than I could handle. But it felt… simple. Like it was the low end of what my magic could do."

"You still haven't gotten it, yet? You have a big heart, Norah, and you fight for the people you care about. You fight for them, and you stop fighting yourself. You let the magic flow freely through you and it leaps to obey."

"You think I don't want it to work during lessons or when I'm practicing?"

"Those are classroom drills. There's no real risk of danger there. But you thrive when the pressure's on. When the stakes are high and every moment matters, you shine. And it's beautiful to watch."

I wished I could believe that. But my shadow magic was dangerous and volatile, and just as chaotic as Micah's magic. And maybe I had stopped doubting myself for a while back there, and just reacted, and maybe that had been why my magic had obeyed… but if I couldn't consciously control it, then I was no safer to be around than he was.

Zachary brushed his fingers along my cheek.

"You're not him," he whispered, as though he could pick the thoughts right out from behind my eyes. "I know your magic still scares you and you think because it's so chaotic it can only bring darkness, but I have only ever seen you use it for good. That's not something someone who's predisposed to evil would do."

"There's just so much I still don't know about my powers. What if they do end up hurting people or dragging me down the same path as Micah?"

"You literally put yourself in the line of fire to protect me." He paused and then added, "Tell me, did you do that knowing your magic was going to protect you?"

"No. Honestly, I figured it was going to be the end. But at least I'd go out knowing I tried to protect someone I cared about."

"There. You're a good person, Norah Sheehan. Far better than a lot of druids I know. The Council better pay attention because you are a force to be reckoned with."

He pulled me in for a tight embrace before I could downplay his words. A smile played across my lips as the words rattled around inside my head. I was a force to be reckoned with. I had to own it, as terrifying as it might be, because if the last two years had proven anything, it was that this world was in serious need of some forceful shifts. I had one more year at Braeseth and for the first time, I was a little sad at the prospect of leaving here next year. I should have seen the signs when I couldn't get rid of my magic last year. The universe didn't want me to be without powers. I had some purpose yet to be discovered.

"Promise me next year will be less stressful, okay? Come by for a date, not an apocalypse," I said, and rested my head on Zachary's shoulder.

"Can't make any promises," he said with a laugh.

No matter what the world threw at me, I knew that with Zachary and Eva by my side, I'd come out the other side. Every challenge my time at Braeseth had thrown at me had made me stronger. A better witch. A better person. I knew it now. My magic wasn't a curse, and it never had been. It may have been shadow magic, but it wasn't dark magic.

It was my destiny, and whatever awaited me next year, I would be ready to face it.

Printed in Great Britain
by Amazon